EYES ON THE ISLAND

EYES ON THE ISLAND

A NOVEL

FRANK REDDY

FICTION ADVOCATE

New York • San Francisco • Providence

A Fiction Advocate Book
© 2016 Frank Reddy
FictionAdvocate.com

Paperback ISBN: 978-0-9899615-3-0
Ebook ISBN: 978-0-9899615-4-7

Cover and interior design by Matt Tanner
Matt-Tanner.com

1 3 5 7 9 8 6 4 2

For Zach Saunders, the world's strongest man

PROLOGUE

September 1, 1992

On his knees, the seven-year-old prayed for his family. For his mom and dad. The little dog next door pacing outside the doghouse. The red roosters with fat muscular legs tied to rusty rebar stakes in the ground. He prayed for the city of Savannah and all the barrier islands. He prayed they would survive this black, swirling mass.

Speaking over the eerily robotic intonations of the weather radio, he chanted the verse. It was his mantra during times like these. The air lit up around him, tiny pixels of strange light that only he could see. He swore to others they were there. He saw them plain as day. The visions, his mom called them. His body grew warm as if steaming bathwater were encircling him.

In his hands, the boy clutched a black Bible. His name glossed the cover: William H. Fordham in gold lettering. It was a Christmas gift from two years prior. Already, the pages showed wear. Highlighted verses and pencil scratches marred the smooth tissue paper. The yellow streaks and graphite marks had made his mother proud.

She hovered above him now, pacing. Turning up the weather

radio. The cold, alien voice grew louder. The syllables didn't connect as they should. The end of each word began promptly with the start of the next. No pause for breath in between. It was unnatural. It sounded like cold metal coming to life. Will imagined the rectangular furnace beside him awakening. Appendages, eyes, teeth, and consciousness as it belched the English language in loud, sober proclamations.

"Saturday-evening. Storm-warning-for-all-in-neighboring counties. Warning extends-to-all-on-the-Georgiacoast. First squall. Thosein-thefollowingcounties. Find shelter. Stayinyourhomes. Second-squall-forecasted-for7:30."

That word. It terrified him. It sounded like the noise something makes before it kills you. "Mommy, what's squall?"

The light flickered above them, a single bulb dangling over the dank crawlspace. The winds picked up outside. The sound of a tree cracking somewhere nearby like a muffled gunshot. There was a dull tumbling above them. "Shh—" the woman said. "Pray for daddy now. Say your verse."

With sweaty palms, he clutched at the Bible. In the face of the storm, it felt small to him. Devoid of power. Squeezing his eyes shut, he chanted the words that calmed him. William Fordham prayed for the wellbeing of his father, who was up on the roof, grappling with a puzzle of big blue tarps, stepping with practiced dexterity across the shingles, strategically placing bricks to weigh them down.

"Peace, be still. Peace, be still. Peace, be still. Peace, be still. Peace, be still."

On the news earlier that night, they'd said it was coming. They'd been saying it for days, but the boy had known about it long before. He could sense it. He could taste it and smell it. The air carried an odor. A red-pulsing warning, which he'd once tried to describe to his mother and father. The couple had looked at each other, not saying a word.

"Peace be still peace be still peace be still peace be still peace be still."

The words ran together now, losing familiarity in the repetition. Each syllable came unhinged to birth a scary, sprawling phonetic marvel. He said the words until he ran out of breath, pausing, looking up at his mother. She shook her head. "He's been up there too long." Then, glancing down at Will: "You wait here."

"Don't leave me."

"You just keep saying your verse."

"No, Mommy. Please don't."

Will shut his eyes as the crawlspace door slammed shut. He bent low, crouching, imagining God: a tall, white-haired man in the sky watching the storm brew. God created hurricanes because men were wicked, his mom had told him. It was during times when Satan moved unchecked in this world that God unleashed his fury. It was a cleansing of sorts. But the storm did not feel like something holy. It felt impersonal. Scary. An explosion of thunder rocked the home's foundation as tears streamed down the boy's face.

"Peace-be-still-peace-be-still-peace-be-still-peace-be-still-peace-be-still."

LOW TIDE

CHAPTER ONE

It started with trembling. The all too familiar.

Will slumped, hunchbacked, toward the church pew as the choir hit high notes. Teeth snapping together, copper taste on his tongue, he plopped down, arms and legs twisted like a stomped spider. His head banged against the pew's mahogany finish.

He felt cold wind blow across his skin. The smells of grape Kool-Aid and pesticide, of stale duplex cookies and bleach, the olfactory remnants of Grace Fellowship Church, disappeared. The off-key a cappella voices of the choir faded, like someone turning the volume down on a stereo.

Dark clouds fast approaching, like television shows with time-lapse photography. Lightning popping, thunder utters a warning, and his fists clench, fingernails breaking the skin: crimson buds bloom on the sanctuary's taupe carpet.

Black and white. Rain patters like prodding fingers against his skull. Undercurrents tug at his legs, writhing tentacles wrapped around the muscles. The sky gone dark and fading as he sinks. Screaming. Woeful shouts like delirious laughter. Dim light fades. A searing pain invading his lungs, his brain.

And then, light. A hand cuts the surface above, plunging toward him, fingers outstretched, beckoning. The hand of a child.

A jolt awoke him where he lay, facedown against the smooth church pew in the tiny sanctuary. He groaned, willing the muscles to move. His arms and legs felt numb as he crawled his way up. His forehead shiny with sweat, he smoothed the cowlick in the back of his blond hair. Will was only thirty, but he felt so much older.

He clenched and unclenched his fists, pushing himself all the way up from the wooden bench. He left sticky palm prints of blood on the varnish. The refinished wood grain reflected light from above. Something about that light, the way it spilled down the slick finish, grounded him. He knew where he was, and he knew he wasn't welcome.

Despite this, he stared down each member of the congregation one by one. Familiar faces darkened. An elder—the one who ceaselessly jingled pocket change—turned away. The widow with the hook nose shoved two sticks of cinnamon gum in her mouth, muttering. The new pastor peered from behind the choir. He offered a sympathetic smile as his wife sobbed into the shoulder of his brand-new suit.

Favor was a fickle thing, Will thought. Back when he was pastor of Grace Fellowship, the congregation fought to say hello to him. They'd quarrel over whose kitchen table he would grace following every sermon. His presence was like God's favor shining down upon them. As he reminisced, Will started to laugh, but it caught in his throat.

An old man appeared at his side.

"William," whispered West Greene, a 70-year-old man with dark skin and white hair. He frowned with paternal worry, inching up beside Will as everyone else watched.

It had been a long time since Will had his last seizure, and he'd nearly forgotten how it felt: the trapdoor opening in his mind, his mouth filling with words he did not understand, his body quaking as the visions came. Yes, visions. That was the best way he could describe them. Like dreaming, but not. The first time he'd had a seizure while preaching—nearly two years ago as he'd stood at the pulpit—the congregation had thought he was playing a trick on them. Others thought he was trying to speak in tongues like one of those Pentecostals. There were those who'd always been suspicious of Will from the start, and this for them was affirmation. He did not belong here.

In the end, they were right, Will thought.

The fingernail cuts in each palm ached as he surveyed the sanctuary one last time. A dozen pews stretched out before him. Each bench holstered three or four mud-colored hymnals, their pages moisture-swollen and stained. The church choir stood frozen, awaiting some cue. Their rendition of "Victory in Jesus" had been cut short by the commotion.

"Have you stopped taking your medication?" West asked.

Will felt better at the sight of West, his mentor and his friend. He blinked. The effects of the seizure were slowly wearing off, all the details coming back to him now. It was Sunday morning, August 2, 2015. One day before his departure.

⬭

The old man spoke with a subtle Geechee accent. The Creole, coastal island cadence was hard to notice except at the beginnings and ends of certain syllables. Not quite foreign, but not quite stateside. The ancestral inflection of West Greene was sanded down, made flush with the English language. As always, it was song to Will as the two stood in the shade behind the church, under a century-old oak tree.

"I don't know why you torture yourself," said West, hot August wind billowing his white shirt. "But I figured you'd be here today."

"It's going to rain," Will said, his voice barely above a whisper. The physical exertion of the seizure had left him drained.

West glanced up toward the cloudless blue sky. The Georgia sun filtered down through oak branches.

Will knelt, grasping a thick vine that roped its way through the turf. He yanked at the noxious weed and took with it a fistful of clover and crabgrass. His ropy forearms bulged as he played tug-of-war with the root system.

West cleared his throat. "You've got to leave it behind."

Will looked up at the old man, this surrogate father figure who'd taught him so much. They'd spent hours upon hours studying the Bible, learning about forgiveness. How to forgive those who'd wronged you. How to find redemption in a world where your friends became your enemies. Every good deed diminished by a horrible, unthinkable twist of fate. None of it seemed to mean anything anymore. Will shook a Camel cigarette out of a soft pack and lit it. "These people," he said. "They'll never let me forget what happened. They'll never forgive me."

"Yes, they've been terrible. It hasn't been easy watching Christian folks act like that. But, God forgives them," West said.

"I've been thinking about God. I've had him wrong this whole time."

Will considered his current state of affairs. He was broke. The landscaping company wouldn't hire him full time. His apartment was a sparsely furnished, three-room shithole on the bad side of Savannah. He still had to pack his meager belongings. He still had to clean. The kitchen counters littered with empty liquor bottles, microwave-dinner containers, and unopened mail, the stovetop with dark rings of soot and brittle scabs of food—just thinking about that stuff made him want a drink so bad. *But no more of that,* he reasoned.

"Maxwell Summerour sent me a letter," West said. "They're expecting you at the pier tomorrow. They're going to give you the whole tour."

"Maxwell Summerour," Will breathed, smoke escaping his mouth. It twisted away in the summer wind. "You ever figure out who he is or what he's doing on your island?"

"It's not *my* island. I haven't been to Muskogee in ages. Too much has changed, and my life is here in Savannah. From what I hear though, they need somebody good. And, this is your way out. You couldn't have planned it better."

"I know. I just got this feeling," Will said. "Like everything has been leading up to this. Not in a good way."

"You saying you don't want to go?"

The ancestors of West Greene hailed from Muskogee, a Georgia barrier island stretching six miles long and two miles wide. The secluded island was accessible only by boat, a courier vessel that ran to and from Savannah once or twice a week. Most of West's relatives had fled the island years ago, moving to small communities around Savannah. With the recent passing of West's uncle, who had served for the past thirty years as the island's pastor, all family ties to Muskogee were cut. And for the first time in three decades, the island needed a new pastor. As the next of kin, West learned of this before anybody else, but he had no interest in taking the job himself. As a grandfather of three, his life was centered on spending time with family in Savannah and continuing his street ministry. On West's recommendation, Maxwell—whose status on the island apparently carried weight—agreed to hire Will effective immediately to fill the post.

Will crushed out the cigarette, pocketing it. He thought about the new pastor of Grace Fellowship. The son of a bitch smiling at him in the sanctuary. The man's arm around his ex-wife, Rose. It wasn't enough that he'd taken Will's job; he'd stolen Will's wife too.

West and Will turned at the sound of voices behind them. People were exiting the church building, going home or heading out to eat with other members of the congregation. Will remembered that. Fellowship after church often felt like a reason to be a Christian in and of itself. Getting a glimpse and being a part of the lives of people who were bound to you by the church. He remembered eating fried chicken and mashed potatoes, brown gravy, meatloaf, chicken pot pie. Listening to mothers bragging on their children, fathers complaining about their children. The thought triggered sadness in his heart, but he pushed it down in the practiced purge of tortured months.

"Who knows?" West said. "You might even get to meet the heiress. That millionaire widow. What's her name?"

"Esther Campbell."

"She's single. Play your cards right, you could inherit Muskogee."

Will smiled, and West laughed.

Minutes passed as the men stood in silence. Will scanned the cemetery. What remained of its integrity came to an abrupt halt one hundred feet away. Gales from the highway sent lotto tickets and McDonald's bags scuttling. Coffee lids and condom wrappers hurtled through the air, dancing in the diesel breath of each surging semi-truck. Most of the litter got trapped in the kudzu that separated the cemetery from the road, vanishing forever beneath blankets of green that swallowed whole trees, their ghostly silhouettes shrouded in chlorophyll. The rest of it landed in the graveyard, blowing among head-stones like distasteful tumbleweeds.

Will got down on one knee, placing a hand on the tiny granite marker. The glossy surface felt strangely cool in the August heat. Will brushed torn blades of crabgrass and clover from the headstone. He concentrated on the meaning of the engraved words before him, the finality as overwhelming as the first time he'd seen it one year ago.

Will said good-bye. They shook hands, West clapping him on the shoulder. Will made his way around the church. His palms ached. They were bleeding again. He wiped them on his pants, crimson streaks. He got in his pickup truck, the lone vehicle in the parking lot. Tears streamed down the cracked vinyl steering wheel. He punched the dashboard, the pain eating him. Why had he come here? In vivid detail, he relived every moment of the funeral, scene by scene. The tiny casket lowered into the earth. He revved the engine. Black smoke poured from the exhaust pipe. *Leave it all behind.*

West knelt at the grave, wiping smeared blood from the granite. He unfolded a handkerchief. "Dark the light," he said.

It was a phrase his grandfather had always used to signify the set-ting of the sun, but there was something else in the words. Something that indicated the strength of unseen forces and the powerlessness of man. He looked down at the small headstone.

AARON JACOB FORDHAM
BELOVED CHILD OF WILLIAM AND ROSE
June 7, 2011–Aug. 2, 2014

Thunder cracked with violence. A wall of dark blue clouds appeared suddenly above the trees.

CHAPTER TWO

Will's hair blew wild in the summer breeze as he crossed the waters that lay between Savannah and Muskogee. The day had a surreal touch to it, the kind of haziness that comes from a lack of sleep. On the courier boat's stern, two weathered flags—USA and Georgia—flapped audibly in the wind. He turned west, watching the Port of Savannah get smaller. The triangles of the Talmadge Memorial Bridge rose over smokestacks and multicolored shipping containers on the mainland.

A vague feeling of relief washed over him as he watched his city diminish in size. The boat rocked in a rhythmic way, which made him drowsy, and for a moment he dozed. The captain's voice startled him.

"Fifteen minutes," the captain said, pointing toward the shadow of dark land welling up on the horizon.

He cut the engine to a lower speed and walked over, wiping his hands on his pants. "Amos McGuire," he said, outstretching his hand. He had a sort of slight, permanent smile and an agreeable disposition that put Will at ease. Will liked Amos immediately.

"You one of those developers?" Amos asked, removing his Braves cap and scratching his balding head.

Will said no.

"Reason I ask," Amos said. "And it's none of my business. Just seems like the only people I take out here anymore is the developers. Assholes, most of them. I drive them out here. Drop them off. Pick them back up." Amos excused himself for a moment and adjusted the throttle. Lighting a cigarette, he shouted over the engine: "I drop them off, and they're in a good mood. I pick them up, and they're all pissed off."

The boat slowed, less than a mile from the sprawling island. Some of its features became clear. A beautiful beach with tiny black specks of driftwood and debris dotted the pristine sands. The jagged tops of palm trees sawed their way into the blue sky.

Will eyed the island, figuring he had time for another cigarette. The captain returned from the helm. "Smoke 'em if you got 'em."

Will smiled. "I'm the new pastor on Muskogee."

"They got a church on that island?" Amos looked surprised, dragging heavily on his cigarette. "How much you know about Muskogee, Reverend? You read the paper?"

Will nodded.

"You remember that Arch Holdings eminent domain mess?"

"Yeah," Will said, recalling newspaper headlines and sound bites from talking heads and politicians. "One thing I never understood, though: If the Port of Savannah wanted Muskogee, and they could legally take it, why didn't they? What stopped them?"

"Hell, what *didn't* stop them?" Amos said, laughing. "For one thing, Department of Natural Resources has laid its claim on Muskogee now. They made some agreement with Esther Campbell that they'll get it for green space when she dies. They're a state agency, and the Port of Savannah is a quasi–state agency. You ain't gonna see two state agencies doing battle over who gets Muskogee. It's bad press. And speaking of bad press, how awful would it look for the Port of Savannah to take an old lady's birthright?"

Will nodded. It was all coming back to him now. Arch Holdings —a steel imports and exports company—had failed many times over the past several years to persuade Esther Campbell to sell her `island, a parcel in a prime spot for developers. Its proximity to the main port had led many other businesses to make offers to the Campbell family heiress as well. Developers had been known to frequent the island, promising huge sums of money in exchange for the property deed. What had set Arch Holdings apart was their persistence as well as political connections to the Port of Savannah. Talks of eminent domain soon surfaced in the Savannah *Daily Post*, and the matter seemed inevitable until an enterprising beat reporter stumbled across damning emails detailing the Port's motives: upon taking possession of Muskogee, the Port would turn around and sell it to Arch Holdings. In damage-control mode, the Port quickly distanced itself from the documents and dropped the issue, removing the island's name forever from its vocabulary.

"Excuse me, Reverend." The captain took the helm again as the waves got choppier. Will removed a final cigarette from his pack and lit it. No more smoking after this. No more booze or medication either. He had to enter this new phase of life with a clear mind, whether his doctor liked it or not. Since ditching the meds, his perceptions had become keen, the sixth sense returning with fresh clarity.

Only four nights earlier, he'd emptied a whole bottle of Carbatrol into the toilet. The aqua blue capsules kept the seizures at bay. Before flushing, he'd poured in his prescription for Klonopin, piss-yellow tablets that countered the panic attacks. He knew that coming off

Carbatrol was a risk. It was more than a risk, really. It was dangerous. But the drug's side effects went beyond nausea and headaches. It was so much worse: The medication dulled those capacities which Will had come to know as an inextricable part of himself, those extrasensory glimpses and unexplainable hunches. On the seizure medication, he felt empty.

The detox had been brief but painful. His body had become used to the drugs, his mind accustomed to the chemicals. Sleeplessness was one of the biggest side effects. His mind was lucid for the first time in nearly a year. The dark thoughts felt real, tangible, as if he could reach out and grapple with them in the darkness. Fanged ghosts sat cross-legged at the foot of his bed.

He'd lain there, sweating beneath the sheets. The thoughts unstoppable, bearing down on him like the heel of something insidious. They were the repressed mind-pictures of his past, and they danced before him when he closed his eyes. He thought of his ex-wife, Rose. He thought of his little boy, Aaron, the child with the curious face. His tiny hands had gripped at Will's larger fingers. The child filled him with fatherly pride, which seemed to spill from his heart stronger than anything he'd ever felt.

As Aaron grew up, the boy had been so full of vitality: running laps around the backyard, giggling with wild abandon at the most mundane observations. He'd watch cartoons on the couch, hugging Will close as he fell asleep. It was a union that made Will's life worth living. If the love of God were real, Will's love for Aaron was surely a reflection.

As the courier boat slowed, approaching the island, gulls shrieked overhead. Will looked up, spotting dark, retreating clouds in the distance. On the previous evening, there had been a raging storm that beat down upon the whole of the eastern coast. He had sensed the front coming on for several days beforehand. It was the old familiar feeling. The approach of something indifferent to his tiny existence. A nebulous presence with unthinkable power. The embodiment of God hundreds of miles away, spreading poisonous tendrils toward him. Not a New Testament God. A God of retribution that terrified him.

The storms were gone now, and the sun warmed his shoulders as the vessel skipped toward Muskogee. Will spotted three figures standing on a pier: a woman, a boy, and a very large man who had what looked like a pit bull on a leash. The woman was waving. All three were darkly tanned. The man was big—more than six foot five with a build. The boy, by contrast, was short and skinny. He looked to be about nine or ten years old. A pair of binoculars hung from the child's neck as he watched the boat approach.

Arriving at the pier, Will realized how beautiful the woman was. Her blue eyes were like nothing he'd ever seen. Her auburn hair seemed to sparkle in the early afternoon sunlight. She wore a pair of tattered shorts, rugged sandals, and a small bikini top. Her large, tan breasts bulged from the ill-fitting garment. Will averted his eyes as he stepped off the vessel.

Helping Will with his luggage—three duffle bags consisting of his sole possessions—Amos gawked without reservation at the woman. "Good luck, Reverend," he said, a wry smile on his face.

Will slung the duffle bag straps over his shoulders, approaching the trio of islanders. He extended a hand toward the huge man, who looked like a linebacker in his prime. He stared at Will, eyes steady. The woman laughed. "He's shy," she said. "It's called a handshake, Frederick."

She put out her own hand instead. "I'm Sally. We're excited to finally meet you. Muskogee hasn't been the same without a pastor." She looked at the boy. "This is my son, John."

The boy looked up. "John, shake Mr. Will's hand," Sally said. The boy offered a weak handshake, eyes darting.

"Nice to meet you, John," Will said to the boy.

John cut a momentary glance toward Sally, twisting his mouth to one side. Sally coughed once. "Ready for the tour?"

Will nodded, feeling Frederick's eyes upon him.

<hr/>

They hiked the main path, a foot-stomped dirt trail lined with large oak trees. Palmettos exploded from the undergrowth, spikes of green fanning out like tail feathers. The jagged plants soaked up what leftover sun they could. The twisted branches and Spanish moss weaved a patchwork blanket of sunlight, which fell upon Will's shoulders as he glanced into the woods. For the hundreds of healthy oaks with robust branches reaching out for sustenance, he happened to notice a single failing tree just beyond the path; yellow lesions striped the trunk and shapeless fungus bubbled from its guts.

The traveling group of four moved swiftly, Will and Sally walking in front while Frederick and John trailed behind. The pit bull nosed along the path beside Frederick. Will chanced a look at Sally. She was beautiful, and there was a sort of otherworldliness to her. Realizing he was staring, she turned and met his gaze. On impulse,

Will nearly looked away, but those eyes held him. Cascading red hair framed her face, falling just below the shoulders. She smiled in a way that shifted all her features into sharper focus, a unifying expression that brought everything together. The effect was powerful.

"Now, did they tell you about our artist colony, how it got started?" Sally said.

She explained how the island had been purchased by the Campbells in the early 1900s. Ownership was passed around, from sibling to sibling, from parent to child, until only one remained: Esther Campbell, who'd married but never had children. After her husband passed away in the early '90s, she'd traveled to Savannah and put the word out about an idea she had: She wanted to establish a small, self-sustaining artist colony. Mirroring her own faith, the group was to be made up of Christians who wanted to create art that reflected the island's natural beauty. For food, they could cultivate and maintain more than twenty acres of already-established vegetable fields. They could hunt the Muskogee hog, a swine that roamed the island in heavy supply. They could live in the slave cabins—stone-and-shell relics which still stood strong from earlier times. Everything was there. And they could stay free of charge, so long as they didn't make trouble.

And so she allowed a handful of artists to come and stay. Some of the artists—about a dozen—had been there now for more than two decades. Some, like John, were descendants of the original artists in the colony.

"But what about the natives?" Will asked.

"Natives?"

"Yeah, like Argus Greene. The guy whose job I'm taking."

She laughed in an embarrassed way. "They didn't really fit in with the plan."

"What do you mean?"

"Well, I guess they didn't like what was going on with the artist colony. They all left."

"Except for Argus."

"He was a good pastor, and he will be missed. But we were past due for a new one. He was—if I'm being honest—insane. I won't go into it, but let's just say he'd lost the faith."

Palmettos rustled up ahead, the fronds knocking together like bones. Will saw a deer leap across the path and, only seconds later, what he thought was an armadillo in the thick undergrowth. The pit bull barked, but Frederick, John, and Sally seemed indifferent.

"Ah, here's Miss Esther's house," she said.

Sally gestured toward a Spanish Colonial Revival–style villa up on a hill, and the group stopped. They walked to the edge of the trail. Will looked at the two-story, sand-colored home with its faded red-tile roof and walls of sun-dried clay.

"It's beautiful, isn't it?" she said, touching Will's arm. He felt it go through him like a warm current. She pointed toward the back of the house, which opened onto a patio and lush flower garden. "That's where we hold opening ceremonies for the pig roast."

"Pig roast?"

"It's only a few weeks away," she said. "You're going to love it. It's our big annual celebration here. It's an old tradition. Plantation owners and slaves used to celebrate the harvest every year. They'd all get together and dance and eat food. The slaves and slave owners each had their own ceremony. The whole idea follows the moon cycles. You'll learn living here how important all that is. The tides are everything."

There was a rustling of paper behind Will, and he turned to see the boy scribbling on a notepad. "Green heron," John said aloud, pushing sweaty bangs from his eyes. He stuffed the small notebook back in his pocket and lifted his binoculars.

Will smiled. "Can I have a look?"

The boy seemed surprised. He looked down at the weathered binoculars and handed them to Will. He pointed toward a swampy body of water. "It's got yellow feet," John said. "Long beak. It's up on the log."

Will squinted into the telescopic glass until he saw the bird, its big eyes darting back and forth. "Very cool. You like birds?"

The boy nodded, hands moving nervously. "I've spotted more than a hundred species here." He took the notebook back out of his pocket and offered it to Will. John's earnest expression, his desire to show off these findings, amused Will. He seemed like a good kid. Being around children usually made Will feel very sad. His tragic past always clouded the joy of it, rising up from the depths if he so much as saw a child. But there was something indefinable about this boy—the innocence, the curiosity, perhaps—that kept Will in the moment. The precise reason for it escaped him. It was much like that parental intuition that guides fathers and mothers to care for their children: It just was. The sudden desire to befriend John seemed similarly ingrained without explanation. Will could feel long-dormant fatherly instincts itching like a phantom limb.

"John, we don't have time for that," Sally said, snatching the notebook. "We've got an appointment. Maxwell is waiting."

John studied the ground and put his hands in his pockets.

"Here you go," Will said, handing the binoculars back to John. "Maybe we can go bird-watching later."

The four continued along the trail for another half mile until they came upon a sprawling field of mostly corn, with several rows of tomatoes and pepper plants. In the distance, a white plantation house stood tall.

"You know, what Maxwell has done here is a big thing," Sally said. "Before he came here, we were all lost."

Sally explained with reverence the occasion of Maxwell's arrival two years prior. She said that upon arriving, he'd spent the entire first day inside his cabin. Nobody knew what he was doing. People waited, wondering why he wouldn't come out. Finally, at dusk, he emerged carrying a tray with more than a dozen intricate ceramic pots. He'd crafted them from a rough mixture of native clay and cooked them over a makeshift firing mound behind the cabin. That night, everybody in the artist colony filled their pots with black drink and stayed up late getting to know this stranger. "It was his gift to us, and he hasn't stopped giving," Sally said.

"What's black drink?" Will asked.

"It's a Muskogee secret. I'll make you some when we get inside."

"How about some ice water?" he asked, wiping his brow.

John appeared at Will's side, trying to keep pace with the adults. "I've never had ice water before," he said.

Sally silenced John with a harsh look. "John's never been off the island. And he's curious about things he doesn't understand. Too curious for his own good."

⬯

Approaching the plantation, they stepped through the gate of an old wooden fence covered in wisteria vines, snaking tendrils interwoven and splintering the wood.

"Y'all got some weeds here," Will said.

Sally stopped. "Wisteria is beautiful when it blooms."

"Yeah, but it will take over. I can help with landscaping if y'all need it. That's what I did before I was a pastor. And after I was a pastor."

"The labor is spread equally among us here," she said, glancing toward the sun. "Maxwell appreciates punctuality. And we're running late."

They climbed a dozen faded brick steps and stopped on the porch. Wooden planks creaked below them. Will looked out across the front yard. The shade trees were old, likely dating back beyond the plantation's construction, but they didn't look like they were going to last much longer. The branches drooped low, heavy with ropy vines. Wisteria as thick as a man's arms girdled the trunks, taking root in the host oak.

Sally knocked at the door. A woman who appeared to be in her midforties answered. She was as lean and tan as Sally, but marked by a facial scar. She wore a ragged T-shirt and blue jean shorts, both smeared with paint. Sally regarded the woman with an expression that was polite yet resembled anger.

Frederick and Sally stepped through the door frame. Will started through the open door, but a small hand tugged at his shirt. He turned and saw John. The boy's eyes moved frantically. Will leaned down, straining to hear his words. "I'm scared," John said, glancing toward the door.

"What is it?" Will said. He looked at the boy, sizing up his facial expression.

John stared intensely at the ground. There a silence that lasted several seconds before he opened his mouth again. "They think I don't know what really happened—"

He was cut off abruptly by the sound of Sally's voice, calling out for the two of them.

The boy pushed past Will, stepping inside the house. Will stood alone on the porch, listening to the sounds of the birds that called and responded to one another. He felt as if a seizure were coming, and his hands began to tremble.

CHAPTER THREE

Maxwell was running late. Very uncharacteristic of him, Sally said. "But there's a lot going on right now," she said. "You've caught us in the middle of preparations for the pig roast."

Feeling ill, Will followed them into the plantation's living room. John turned around, looking toward Will for a brief moment. He wondered what the hell the boy had been trying to tell him. John had seemed so terrified out on the porch, eyes moving as if surrounded by invisible enemies. Will watched Sally place a hand on John's shoulder, then lean toward Frederick, whispering. The large man suddenly grabbed John by the arm, leading him out the front door. "They've got an errand to attend to," Sally explained.

She asked Will to have a seat as she stepped out of the room. Gladly, he collapsed onto an old couch. It creaked sickeningly as he fell upon it. Will felt like he was going to pass out. A seizure seemed imminent. He closed his eyes, taking short breaths through his nose, a trick the doctor had once taught him.

The home was expansive and dark. Heavy-looking, burgundy-colored curtains blocked the daylight except for a single finger of sun, which stretched across the wooden floor, touching the tip of Will's sneakers. The few remaining original furnishings—a gilded mirror over a cherrywood console table, mahogany chaise lounge with butter-yellow cushions, Victorian-style striped sofa—were scratched, cracked, or splintered. The rest of it was a mishmash of antique furniture. It seemed nothing in the room had been refinished or refurbished since its manufacture. A sad teak rocking chair looked diseased, overtaken by some kind of black mold. The contents of a showcase in the corner hid behind dirty glass. The whole room was filled with outdated clothing, all draped and hung from pieces of furniture. Robes, thrift-store T-shirts, corduroy pants. A dull-colored necktie dangled from a stationary ceiling fan. Thick dust coated everything.

Will stood, the couch creaking again beneath him. He walked across the wooden floor, which also groaned under his weight. The house had a musty smell to it, like an indoor flea market, but there was something foul too. Like rotten meat. He took his steps carefully, still feeling uneasy and quite possibly on the verge of a seizure.

"Sally?" he said. What would he do, and how would he explain it? The people who knew Will, really knew him, had memorized the proper procedure. Flip him on his side. Move furniture and anything harmful out of the way. Let it pass, then check for injuries. Use a finger to gently clear his mouth of vomit.

His ex-wife, Rose, had been through it countless times. She could do it in her sleep. But Sally would likely have no idea what was going on. He'd sprawl out on the floor helpless, choking on his lunch. Sally might even get to witness him chew off his own tongue, a squirming, bloody muscle at her feet as she returned from the kitchen.

He shut his eyes, focusing again on the breathing exercise. After several minutes, the weakness passed.

"I'll be right out," Sally said, shouting over the sound of pots and pans clattering, of water hissing. Will noticed a picture framed above the door. The artwork featured a group of dark-skinned men sitting in a semicircle on nine large stone benches, stars dotting the sky. One of the men was handing something like a small cup to another. The painted moon seemed to glow through the glass. Its preternatural illumination almost seemed lit by means of electricity.

"That's an original painting," Sally said. She came out of the kitchen holding two ceramic mugs, each steaming. "It's called *Island of the Black Drink*. See the stones the natives are sitting on? That's the Crescent, which is one of our rarest features here. If you ask Maxwell, he might take you down there. It's just a short walk from the house here. But you have to check with him, because normally it's off-limits."

He wondered why it would be off-limits, but decided not to pry. "So who painted this picture?"

She handed Will one of the mugs. "No idea. It's really old, though. Piece of shit, if you ask me."

"Wow, opinionated."

"Well, as a painter, I can look at this and see all the little flaws that others might not notice, so I'm overly critical. It's easy for me to notice when someone takes shortcuts in their work."

"What kind of painting do you do?"

"Oil painting mostly," she said. "How's your black drink?"

A bitter aroma rose from the cup of liquid, which looked like flat Coca-Cola. "What's in it?" Will asked.

"It's crushed-up leaves of the yaupon holly. It's a native plant on Muskogee."

He brought the steaming cup to his lips and tasted the earthy, bitter black drink. It was unbearably strong. The astringent liquid nearly made him gag.

"I think it tastes like herbal medicine," Sally offered. "It's got a lot of caffeine, which is nice."

"It's interesting."

"You don't have to like it," she said, laughing. "I just thought you should try it. It's such an important part of this island's history."

A door opened and closed behind them.

"Libations of our natives," said a man of medium height wearing khaki pants and a white button-up shirt. He wore a bright smile and had penetrating blue eyes. "I myself prefer something stronger."

<hr/>

For a man who appeared to be more than three decades older than Will, Maxwell Summerour moved fast. He spoke with a speedy rhythm which left his listeners leaning forward, trying to catch every last syllable. The two men entered Maxwell's office, a meticulously clean room with a large open window. "Please have a seat," Maxwell said, gesturing toward a metal folding chair. "Apologies for such rudimentary furnishings."

Maxwell plucked a glass bottle from the shelf beside his desk. He removed two mugs from a drawer and poured two good-sized glugs of clear liquid. Leaning over his desk, Maxwell handed one of them to Will. "Cheers."

Will had a near physical reaction to the fumes rising from the cup. It was pungent as rubbing alcohol. After nearly a year plumbing the depths of full-on alcoholism, he felt an emotional connection to the smell. The last couple days of clean living had been a struggle, but his resolve had been unyielding. The temptation in his hands now broke him in two. And he didn't want to be rude. Will raised the cup to his lips. The liquid felt like a thousand tiny needles pricking his tongue. He could feel the warmth in his throat, then his stomach, followed by a fuzzy euphoria he knew all too well.

"Moonshine," Maxwell said, taking a seat. "From homegrown corn. We've had a good crop the last couple of years. Big, beautiful stalks of Silver Queen. Have you seen the cornfields? They're a point of pride for us here. We've really come a long way. Another?"

Will shook his head. Maxwell poured himself a second.

"When I get the chance, I'll show you how we make this stuff. A very precise process, making moonshine. We've got a still out there in the woods next to the old shed. Oh my God, it was a revelation when we found that shed. Like discovering buried treasure. All kinds of farm equipment, you know. All of it old. Even older than me." He laughed. "Then, there's the matter of—"

Will tried to keep up with the man as he jumped from subject to subject. He felt buzzed from the little swallow of moonshine. It was powerful stuff. It felt good. It had been several days since he'd had so much as a beer, and he welcomed the momentary tranquility.

"—from a tradition," Maxwell continued. "We worked hard so that we could make our way in this world. My mother was right. Nothing that's worth a damn comes easy. Take these people for instance. The artists of Muskogee."

Maxwell lowered his voice and gestured for Will to close the door. "A bunch of spoiled rich kids," he continued with a conspiratorial smile. "I mean, let's be honest here. These artists came to this island in search of what they'd been missing all their lives: the exhilaration of survival and thriving, which can only be attained through hard work. When I arrived here, foolishly, I expected to find people like myself who take pleasure in their art but also understand the importance of discipline.

What was it Jack London said? 'You can't wait for inspiration. You have to go after it with a club.' These artists were languishing, Will. Their art suffered. These were a people who needed discipline. These were a people who needed direction. I offered them both." He stopped, and then he smiled. "Lord, I'm rambling. Sorry. All that to say...from what West Greene told me, you sound like the kind of guy we want around here: a hard worker."

"West is a good guy," Will said. "And I really do appreciate y'all giving me a chance."

There was a knock at the door. Will turned around to see Sally. She held a platter of smoked mussels, wedges of plump red tomatoes, and a hunk of meat deep-fried beyond recognition. The aroma was intoxicating. Will's mouth watered. "Your favorite," she said, setting the plate down in front of Maxwell.

"Ah, yes. Thank you. Now, Will, if you'll excuse me I'm going to take my dinner in the office here. Sally can show you the way out."

Will stood, outstretching his hand, but Maxwell's eyes were fixed on his food. He leaned into the steaming plate, inhaling deeply through his nostrils. With bare hands, Maxwell grabbed the deep-fried brick of animal flesh and tore into it. Slimy strips of meat slid from his fingers as he gnawed, grease running down his chin. He looked up. Maybe it was Will's imagination, but he felt suddenly that he was looking at a completely different person. It was unsettling. The gloss of civility slipped as Maxwell chewed. Without ceremony, he spit gristle into a napkin and picked up a tomato wedge. He ate it whole, a rivulet of pink juice streaming from the corner of his mouth.

Sally took Will by the arm, leading him downstairs.

They stepped out on the porch, the late afternoon sounds of the island overtaking them. Bugs making music in the trees. Strange-sounding birds screaming. Sally walked to the edge of the steps and smiled.

"He must have been starving," Will said.

"Maxwell forgets his manners," she said. "And he loves his fried gator. Frederick just brought one back fresh this morning. Big one. We've got enough for breakfast if you want some."

Will pictured Frederick, remembering the cold stare. "He hunts alligators?"

"Frederick is very talented. Animal instincts. He does all of the hunting here."

"You and Frederick, y'all are—" Will stopped himself, realizing he was overstepping. The moonshine had loosened his tongue.

"Together?"

"It's none of my business," Will said.

"No, no, it's okay. It's complicated, I guess you could say. On Muskogee, we try not to put labels on everything."

She squeezed his arm, and they walked together toward the cabin.

<hr>

The structure was in better shape than he'd expected. Built of sand, lime, and oyster shells, the slave cabins had stood strong over the years. As they approached Will's cabin, Sally pointed toward the faded streaks of eggshell blue along the door frame and above the windows. She said that when actual slaves inhabited the buildings, they'd applied "haint blue" paint above doorways and across windowsills. Will had seen the color many times before on shutters and doors back in Savannah. They walked inside. Will's cabin, she explained, was the only one with glass in the window frames and pine floorboards instead of dirt.

The glass had been installed several years back as an experiment to keep the bugs out, but it hadn't made a difference because there was no longer a front door. A huge mosquito landed on Will's arm as she talked. Sally slapped it, leaving a bloody splotch. "Sorry," she laughed.

The cabin was cozy, not much bigger than an average-sized bedroom. There was a fireplace on one side of the cabin. There was a nightstand and a chest of drawers. In the middle of the room was a bed, its metal frame corroded by saltwater mists. Resting atop it was a discolored mattress with no sheets. Sally sat down on the bed, silently looking Will in the eyes.

The moment may have lasted five minutes. It may have lasted a matter of seconds. But it was a sequence of time that distinctly set itself apart from what preceded it. She stopped talking. Will stopped listening. They shared this loaded silence. She ran her hand along the mattress, caressing the material with slender fingers. He took a few steps toward the bed, the pine floor popping beneath his sneakers. He still had the duffle bags slung over his shoulders. He set them down.

Those eyes again. Her shoulders and chest rising and falling so subtly with each breath. Her tan skin the color of gold in the waning light. She still had on the tiny bikini top. The shorts that barely covered her. He wanted her so badly, but was this wrong? *Flee from sexual immorality. All other sins people commit are outside their bodies but those who sin sexually are sinning against their own bodies.* He struggled to remember the rest of the verse. Something about honoring God because you are not your own. What did sexual immorality mean anyway? It could mean anything. What a wide-open statement that was. He'd skirted the issue many a time during his sermons because he simply didn't believe sex before marriage was a sin. It was a misconception—and for some reason one that nobody would readily admit—that the Bible specifically condemned sex before marriage. Was it a bad idea? Sometimes. A sin? No. But for the time being, Will realized, he didn't give a shit either way. He sat down on the mattress. Out of nervous habit, he smoothed the blond cowlick on the back of his head.

Sally leaned back, resting elbows behind her. Her hair spilled down the contours of her shoulders. "You know, you've got a really beautiful face," she said. "You look so innocent, boyish."

Will laughed. "Don't let that deceive you."

"I'd like to paint you sometime. Portraits are my specialty."

"I think I'll pass," he said.

"Oh, come on. It'll be fun. I can bring my easel and put it right over there. There's some pretty decent light in here." She furrowed her brow. "It sounds crazy, but you actually remind me of my late husband."

"I didn't realize you were married before."

"How could you have known?" she smiled. "What about you?"

He nodded. "Six years."

"My husband passed away a while back. It's been a few years."

"John's father?"

She nodded. "What about you. Did you have children?"

"My son, Aaron—there was an accident. Rose, my wife, she said what we had together wouldn't work anymore. She left me for someone else. Another pastor actually."

"Oh my God. When was this?"

"It was a year ago. We were on the beach and something happened. I couldn't—" Will hesitated. It was too much to lay on her, and who was she anyway? Why was she so interested in him? They'd known each other for a matter of hours. What was this woman he'd just met doing on his bed? Was it that lonely here on Muskogee? He began to feel wary. He'd made the mistake before of being too trusting with people, and he wasn't going to be so naïve this time. "I'm tired," he said. "It's been a long day."

———

The mosquitoes buzzed at his ear. Will tossed and turned, cursing at the tiny insects. It was enough to drive a man insane, but deep down, he knew it wasn't the bugs. He was mad at himself. The past continued to eat away at his life, ruining anything good. Moving to Muskogee hadn't changed a thing. Wasn't this the whole reason he'd come out here? Put distance between himself and the past. Spend time on this quiet island. Start fresh in a place that in no way resembled Savannah. Figure out why God would give him everything, only to take it all away. Give God a chance to explain himself.

Much as it had for the past several nights, sleeping seemed an impossible task. He shifted positions. What he wouldn't give for his medication. The yellow pills calmed his nerves. They dispatched the horrifying memories. The more he tried not to think about it the more the past invaded his neural network. He closed his eyes, breathing deeper, and finally gave in, letting it all come full force.

The sky is blue, ocean cresting foamy white suds as he stands waist-high in the warm, salty water. Aaron bounces up and down, his tiny body squeaking against a clear plastic inner tube. The sound of the tube makes him laugh. Dunking his head, Will moves underwater toward his son. Springing up from the waves, Will explodes from the water surface. The child squeals with laughter. Will turns toward the beach. Rose lies motionless on a maroon towel with a tropical tree pattern. She is asleep. An eruption of laughter as the boy punches at the water. They share a smile. Father and only son. This tiny version of himself whom he loves so much. Will stares into the familiar eyes, the green so much like his own. He looks at Aaron's thick blond hair, matted with salt water. Then he turns his back on the boy.

—

A crunching sound awoke him. He watched the door frame, wondering what nocturnal things lurked in Muskogee woods. He took hold of the side of the bed, pushing himself up from the mattress, wincing as it squeaked. The white noise of insects overtook the night. He eased himself off of the bed, slipping on his sneakers. Will crept toward the door frame, scraping his knuckles along the rocky wall.

Outside, the moon lit up the sandy path like a luminescent trail between twin walls of darkness. He blinked, and then, suddenly, the world was made up of a billion pixels. Like the microscopic dots on a television screen, they all converged to create a whole. His legs trembled. His body ached. Something hit Will like a gust of wind, nearly toppling him. He sucked in the air. It felt painful but somehow orgasmic. He stumbled off the porch and collapsed in the sand, mouth agape, awaiting the inevitable visions.

Will stared up at the sky, seeing the capillaries of the universe. Grains of sand beneath his fingers melded together, forming a supple wave that thumped through his body like a heartbeat. The rhythm of the wind, the chanting cicadas, the far-off whisper of ocean waves began to harmonize, complementing one another, and it sounded like the respirations of God. It was beautiful. It was love.

And then, everything changed.

A distinct chill started at the base of his spine. It ran up his neck like icy fingers. The sounds grew louder, the pulsing light stronger. Thumps from the ground like the beating of a bass drum. The vibrations ran through his body and exploded into the sky in pulsing strobes of ever-increasing intensity. The source of all of this was somewhere beyond the horizon, moving toward this island like a hideous night-mare. Coming for him. Coming for all of them. *We're all connected by this network, and this is an important place. We are in an important place.* The voice in his head felt like a radio transmission. It was monotone, drained of the faintest hint of emotion. It was that uncaring intonation. That absence of humanity. Something old and rusted and dreadful making steady progress to this place. Stretching toward him. Never-ending gears, all connected as one. Yes, there is a God. No, he doesn't care. God isn't a watchmaker. God is a watch.

This is hallowed ground.

———

He blinked, and it was all gone without a trace. It was merely nighttime. He was merely on an island in the Atlantic. The mosquitoes swarmed his skin. The vivid details of the experience began to fade almost immediately. These wide-awake glimpses were always fleeting upon his return. By the next morning, he'd likely remember only the most basic details.

And there it was again. That sound. It sounded like someone nearby kicking gravel.

He felt exposed to the elements, to the whims of whatever moved about in the brush. In a matter of hours it would all be light, the sun rising above the sparkling waters that surrounded Muskogee. But right now he could hardly see a thing. The breeze whipped at him sharply. It was a cool wind for August. Palm trees swayed all around him. Beyond the gangly tree trunks, the forest birthed dark apparitions. Silhouettes of untamed growth rustled. An unnavigable tangle of flora hid mysteries beyond his comprehension. The forest floor itself a graveyard of religion. Roots, soil, and time grinding up the bones of voodoo priests, shamans, and Christian men alike.

Someone coughed. Will froze.

A burst of breeze rustled the saw palmetto fronds, the rigid spikes tapping together. Will took a step forward. It seemed the sound had come from directly in front of him. He moved slowly, eyes shifting toward the source. He could see the vague silhouette of a human figure standing there, just a few yards away, body obscured by the forest's shadows.

"Sally?" he said.

The shape moved, followed by a sound like stifled laughter. The figure swayed beneath the black foliage, snapping twigs. Whoever or whatever was lumbering toward him looked big. Will surveyed the ground, looking for a rock or a large stick. Was it Frederick? That enormous bastard stalking him, spying on him, jealous of Sally's interest in him. Finding no weapon, Will balled his hands into fists. "Don't come any closer."

The figure shrank away.

He waited. Wind blew at the clouds, revealing a luminous crescent moon in the purple sky. The air carried an alien funk, like matted animal fur and decomposition. The entire night was filled with paranoia. Unfounded, perhaps. Was this all part of the same strange hallucination? He entered the cabin, feeling overwhelmed.

There was someone sitting on the bed.

CHAPTER FOUR

Will followed John through the woods. They'd been walking for several minutes now, and Will's eyesight had yet to fully adjust to the night. John, on the other hand, hurried along a dozen paces ahead as if he could see quite well in the dark, dodging low-hanging tree limbs and hurdling felled logs in a fluid fashion.

When Will had entered the cabin only moments earlier to find John sitting there on the bed, still as a statue, the boy had said only one thing: "There's something you need to see."

He was tired and didn't feel like following this boy through treacherous terrain in the middle of the night. What time was it anyway? He had no clue. No clocks to be found on Muskogee. But in truth, the chances of him getting sleep tonight were slim anyway, and his curiosity got the better of him.

He and the boy clipped along at a rapid rate. There was something nostalgic about all this: nocturnal adventures through the forest. Aaron used to lead Will through the woods behind the house. The little boy taking his hand with sticky popsicle fingers. The two of them crashing through the woods in search of "buried treasure." It did not feel unlike that as he and John trekked toward this unknown destination.

But as Will moved blindly through the brush, he thought about the alligators. Stepping over plants that stabbed at his legs, hobbling on uneven ground that bent his ankles as he tried to keep up, he couldn't help but wonder how safe all this was—namely, for the boy. "Does your mom know you're out this late?" Will asked.

The boy shushed him. "They're going to hear us."

His eyes began to adjust. He glanced toward the night sky. He could see the twisted branches of oak trees reaching up for the light. They looked like malformed appendages, making a diabolical lattice-work of the canopy above. And the air was thick. Saltwater mist clung to his clothing. Will didn't mind the outdoors. He found nature to be a renewing force, a respite in which to clear his mind. But there was something menacing about this island at nighttime. He took each step carefully.

They stopped at a clearing. "It's at the end of that path," John said, pointing out a barely visible trail through the woods. At either end of the path, the hunched figures of bushes and shrubs swayed in the breeze. Where the hell was this kid taking him?

"We're close to the plantation," Will guessed.

"We're behind it," the boy said.

"What's down there?"

"The beach."

"But the beach is back that way," Will said, confused.

"No, this is the other beach. The one you don't know about."

Will could feel the ground getting steeper. He panted, sucking in the salty air. He was out of shape. By appearance, he was lean and muscular. The daily toil of landscaping work had made him stronger than most men, but the alcoholism had cost him his health. It was payback for the daily abuse of his body. You couldn't live like that—a pint of Jameson and a six-pack of beer every night. Two packs of cigarettes a day. As he wheezed, trying to keep up with John, Will vowed to get stronger.

The trail ended at the edge of a small cliff, which overlooked the beach and the ocean. As soon as they exited the forest, the night became much brighter, moonbeams shining down on them. "You can sit down," John said. He pointed toward two rocks which had been slid together in the shape of a bench. Will sat. The boy crouched before another rock on the ground beside them. He pushed against it, and it slid easily—too easily.

John cleared the dirt and brush beneath where the rock had been. He turned to Will. "Can you see the people down there?"

Will scanned the shore. This wasn't the main beach that he'd seen on his way into Muskogee. It was indeed a different one, tucked away on the opposite end of the island, which meant that was the Atlantic he was looking at. The sprawling ocean—thousands of miles of salt water—stretched out before him. It went on forever. The next mass of land was Africa, he figured. That seemed insane. But then again, Africa seemed about as far away as Savannah right now. Come to think of it, Muskogee felt like another planet, spinning somewhere on the outskirts of its very own solar system.

"Use these," John said, handing over his binoculars. "Look past the tide pool."

Will looped the leather strap around his neck. It was a small beach, maybe a hundred yards long. He squinted through the scratched glass. "I don't see anything." "Keep looking."

He could see the surf crashing. The ground in some places seemed to writhe. Steadying the binoculars, he saw armies of ghost crabs crisscrossing the sand, their yellow-white shells reflective in the moonlight.

The crustaceans swarmed the corpse of a big fish; Will thought it might be a red drum.

Just beyond that, he noticed someone standing in the surf. Will focused the binoculars on a swath of beach skirting the edge of a massive tide pool. Nearby, there was an unusual-looking formation of large rocks in the sand. Like some variation on Stonehenge. Will blinked, making sure he wasn't imagining it. The boulders were huge, each the size of a park bench. He counted nine of them, forming a semicircle just like the one he'd seen on the painting inside the plantation house. The formation's open end faced the ocean.

He realized at once it was Maxwell standing ankle deep in the surf. Several people—one of them Will recognized as Sally—sat on the rocks. "I see them," Will said.

The boy continued sweeping dirt from the spot on the ground where the rock had been. His efforts revealed three rotten planks. John removed them carefully, stacking them beside the hole in the ground. Will could smell the damp earth underneath. From the hiding place, John removed a Tupperware container the size of a shoebox. He sat down, opening it.

"What is that?" Will said, curious at the great lengths the boy had gone in hiding it.

"That's the Crescent down there," John said, changing the subject "The big rocks in a half circle. I'm not allowed to go. I'm not even supposed to talk about it. The whole beach is off-limits to everyone except when they're having the meetings."

"What are they doing?"

John started to speak but stopped, the corner of his mouth twisting. "I had to go to bed early tonight. That's how I knew they were meeting. They only meet once or twice a month. Not everybody.

Usually just Maxwell, Sally, and Frederick. Sometimes I see other people down there." John snapped open the Tupperware lid, lunar light illuminating its contents: a stack of papers and photographs held together by rusty paper clips.

From his pocket, the boy removed a large lock-blade pocketknife. He flicked it open in a practiced motion. The tip glimmered in the moonlight.

"Nice knife," Will said.

"It was my dad's," John said. "This was his favorite. He used to tell me it was one of a kind."

John placed the knife in Will's hand. It was large and heavy. He examined the bone-colored handle. Will recalled his own first knife, which his father had given him when he was about John's age. It was a cheap one with a black plastic handle, but he loved it nonetheless. He whittled sticks he found in the front yard. He stabbed holes in the lawn, blade sinking to the hilt. Having a knife when you were a boy, it made you feel strong. The sound of it clicking open made a boy feel like a young man. Will folded it shut and handed it back to John.

"He gave it to me before he died. I found all this other stuff in the big house," John said, looking in the direction of the plantation home. "I found a secret way into Maxwell's room, through the crawl space."

John's words were alarming. Will began to wonder how much of what he was hearing was made up. If it wasn't all lies, there was something very strange going on.

Will eyed the stack of yellowed paper. "It's all my dad's old writing," John said. Will picked up the stack of paper. At the top of the first page, he read: "*Island of the Black Drink* by Howard Mansell."

Will squinted at the first few paragraphs. The documents seemed to offer a brief history of the island.

"I've got everything he saved here," John said. "He was a nature writer, but he wrote something else too. For the newspaper." John handed Will a paper-clipped stack of frail news clippings from the Savannah *Daily Post*. Each contained a grainy photo of Howard Mansell at the top next to the column's name, "Eyes on the Island." A sudden gust of wind nearly sent the papers flying.

John removed several photographs. "You want to see him?"

"How old were you—"

"When he died? I was six. I remember him really well. I dream about him sometimes. That he comes to rescue me."

"From what?"

"Let me see the binoculars."

Will placed them in John's hands. "I guess these were his too."

John crept toward the very edge of the drop-off. "Dad couldn't get to the beach. He was in a wheelchair," he said, raising the binoculars. "His wheelchair would always get stuck in the sand if he tried to get down there. So he made this trail. He used to watch from up here." John leaned closer still to the edge of the nearly thirty-foot drop.

"Hey, be careful," said Will.

John retreated several steps, annoyed. "I'm fine."

Will flipped through the old photos, squinting in the dark. He could make out the image of a man on a beach, arm draped over a woman in a bikini. It was Sally, a much younger Sally. She was wearing a similar ill-fitting bikini top. The man in the photo wore sunglasses, a cigarette hanging from the corner of his smile.

He flipped to the next picture. It was a formal head shot of Howard Mansell in a military uniform, a dozen medals pinned to his shirt, including the Purple Heart. "Your dad, he was a hero in the army? That's pretty cool."

"Yeah."

Will tried to make out the man's features in the dark. "And that's why he was in the wheelchair?"

"He was ambushed," John said.

Howard Mansell had blond hair, green eyes, broad shoulders, a tan complexion. He carried an ever-alert, earnest expression. Will bent toward John, moonlight illuminating the photo.

"Your dad, he uh—" Will wasn't sure how to say it without sounding vain or foolish, but it was obvious. Will Fordham and Howard Mansell looked enough alike to be twin brothers.

He handed Will the binoculars and took the photos back, placing them inside the Tupperware container. What was it about this kid? He couldn't figure out why, but John's paranoia was rubbing off on him. John just seemed so, well, sincere about it all. It was if the boy were pitted against the inhabitants of the entire island, and he'd gone renegade with these secret Tupperware boxes and binoculars. And then there were these allegedly clandestine beach meetings.

Will looked through the binoculars. From this vantage point, he could clearly see Maxwell, arms reaching out toward the others as they watched him from the rocks.

John handed Will the Tupperware box. "Don't tell anybody I told you this."

"What?"

"Do you promise you won't tell?"

Will nodded.

"My dad used to tell me there was no such thing as God. But I believe now," John said, eyes filling with tears. "I believe in God because I believe in the devil."

Will put a hand on John's shoulder. "Hey, what's wrong?"

49

"I'm scared."

"Why are you scared?"

"They think I don't know," John continued. "But I saw what they did to Pastor Argus."

"What do you mean?"

John wiped at the tears. He drew a ragged breath. "They're murderers."

CHAPTER FIVE

On Will's first Sunday morning as Muskogee's pastor, he felt nervous. Walking the trail toward the old church, he did his best to dissolve the doubts that ate away at him. He wanted for this to work, for God to reveal himself, so that he might give these people a reason to believe. For that to happen, though, he himself would have to believe.

But the more he tried to concentrate on the sermon and on his reason for being here on Muskogee, the more he felt distracted by the boy's words from several nights back. Will had dismissed them at first as the manufactured musings of an imaginative boy with too much time on his hands. Will himself had been full of imagination as a boy. Being an only child often did that to young minds. Plus kids just said off-the-wall stuff in general.

As Will walked, he prayed and surveyed the flora. Wisteria left a trail of choked tree skeletons in its path, a stripped forest of brittle palm fronds and husks. Will looked at the vines, which seemed to writhe and twist before his very eyes. The root systems of the plants were thick and looked to be decades old in some places. Spent seedpods dangled from bright green leaves. Skinny green lizards skittered along in the underbrush. It was a strangely cool morning, the path shaded by the tall oaks and their big branches. He breathed in the fresh air, stepping carefully so as not to scuff the only good pair of dress shoes he owned.

Will was rusty and he knew it. Bottled up for too long inside his heart, the scriptures and quotes no longer came easily. There had been a time during his mentorship with West when his spirituality flourished. His faith was solid. West called it "preaching from the heart, not the pulpit." It was like riding the crest of unstoppable momentum, a feeling he'd not experienced for some time.

Will stopped at a clearing, peering at a swampy inlet of brackish water. Neon green algae bloomed, sealing the water's surface like a tomb. Tall blades of grass lay crushed flat in a wide path, a straight swath into the murky water made by what was likely a very large reptile. He watched the surface, hoping for a glimpse, a physical manifestation of the mud-colored beast. It was that which he could not see—could not size up—that made him uneasy. His bouts with bad luck—yes, that's what it was, bad luck—were quantifiable now. He could look back on the past year and recount the most awful of events, but at least he could put a name on them: a dead son, a wife who no longer loved him. *If God is not real, and there is no plan to make sense of all this in the end, then what's stopping the bad luck from coming again? From never stopping until it's all over?*

He flipped open his Bible to the book of Isaiah, chapter 43. A message of redemption. He felt unsteady, unsure of himself. He felt the need to lean heavily on something simple yet solid.

He walked among the many wonders of a natural paradise and yet lived in such a state of inescapable gloom. The chains that followed Will Fordham bit into his ankles, clinking behind him no matter where he went, no matter how beautiful, how serene the landscape. In lucid moments of profound sadness, Will realized he could travel the world and never escape the sickness that gnawed at the flesh of his heart.

But there was something else. Something beyond what he'd come to expect. It seemed to lurk, stemming somehow from the boy's revelations. Whether believable or not, Will had taken the words to heart. There was a presence on the island, a germ of something not quite right. It was a force unlike anything he'd ever felt. Maybe this was why Will was here. Maybe it wasn't about him at all.

He wanted to be able to comfort the boy, the only human being on Muskogee he might actually be able to help. The souls of these people felt lost—no, indifferent. He looked at the few islanders he'd met as an extension of Maxwell. It was as if they were not occupying individual bodies but rather hollow human shells. Even Sally. Despite the feelings of desire she stirred within him, there was something missing. Her own son even seemed wary of her, as if his mother were a stranger.

"Hello, sweetheart."

The voice startled him, and he turned to see a woman who looked to be in her late sixties making her way toward him.

"It's beautiful, isn't it?" said Esther Campbell, gesturing toward the waters. "My husband, God rest his soul, always used to laugh when I said that. But I always thought the algae was so pretty. Nothing else in the world is that green." She approached Will, eyes moving up and down him. "Well, my goodness. Are you the new pastor? You are so handsome." The corner of her mouth twisted suddenly into a frown. "You look familiar."

⎯⎯

They walked together. Despite her age, Esther seemed quite youthful. Her face was handsome, and she spoke with a steady ease. She pointed out various trees, birds, and landmarks that she held dear. Her excitement was hard to contain with the introduction of each solitary nuance. She seemed to be living vicariously, as if she too were seeing much of it for the first time. "You'll have to forgive me," she said, gripping his arm as they stepped in time with each other. "I don't get a lot of visitors. I must seem very lonely and sad to you. The only people who visit anymore are the damn developers."

"I heard they're pretty persistent," Will said.

"Oh, you don't know the half of it. I thought I was going to have to get a restraining order for those Arch Holdings scoundrels. They'd show up on the island all the time, unannounced. They even tried to take it away from me. They went and talked the Port of Savannah into stealing Muskogee. That's legal, can you believe it?"

"The eminent domain stuff?"

She nodded. "Just because I'm old doesn't make me a fool. Everything you see around you, it's going to belong to the Department of Natural Resources one day. I want everyone to be able to enjoy this island when I'm gone. Like a big public park."

They approached the old church. It was the first time he'd seen it, and he was instantly fascinated by the tiny foursquare building. Its bright red door and faded, crimson metal roof. White paint blistered and peeled, flaking at the corners where the wood had rotted. A church bell was mounted on the rooftop. "Your first Sunday sermon," she said, handing him the church bell's cord. "You do the honors."

Will grasped the weathered cord and yanked. The bell rang loudly, its volume surprising.

"Everybody on the whole island can hear it, no matter where they are," Esther said, a touch of pride in her voice.

They stepped inside the church. The wooden floors groaned beneath his weight, popping and cracking, sending echoes throughout the tiny sanctuary. He ran his hands along a battered pew as he stepped down the aisle, the scent of mildew heavy. Esther coughed, clearing her throat. "We need to air this out once in a while," she said. "Of course, it's been months since anybody's been inside. That poor old pastor. He would have kept preaching till the day he died if he could."

"Argus Greene?"

She nodded. "You know him?"

"I know his nephew, West."

"Argus lost his mind. Alzheimer's, we think. Started talking to himself. Chasing demons around the island. Cussing out trees and talking to the ghost crabs and alligators. Poor Argus."

Will made his way to the pulpit. He stepped onto the stage, which rose half a foot higher than the rest of the sanctuary. He set his Bible down on the pulpit and observed the empty pews. The windows on each side of the church—three on the left and three on the right—had been whited out with paint. The sun filtered in, casting a fuzzy incandescence on all things. It made the sanctuary feel hazy, as if part of a dream.

Esther took a seat in the front row and dug into her purse, searching for something. She took her Bible out of the large bag, opening it and removing a bookmark. "So good to have a man of God here," she said. "I love a good sermon."

Will opened his Bible, taking out a sheet of paper upon which he'd scribbled some notes. There was a time when he didn't need notes. It all just flowed from somewhere inside. But that had been a long time ago, and it seemed the more he thought about it, the more distant that time felt. As if his past were all part of a stranger's life and had nothing to do with his own.

Others walked into the church as he flipped through the Bible. The woman with the scarred face whom he'd seen briefly at Maxwell's plantation walked in with a balding, middle-aged man. The man had been introduced to Will as "the Teacher." He seemed annoyed to be there. Another couple came in, loudly arguing. Their voices did not decrease in volume until Esther gave them a look. Four or five others came in too, sitting down or lingering about the pews. They were all dressed in T-shirts and shorts. Their whispers filled the tiny room.

"How can he just sit there and tell me his lies?" one of the women said to another. "He knows I'm just going to figure it out."

"It took us almost two hours, but we got it taken care of," one of the men said to another. The other man crossed his arms, nodding.

The scene did not feel utterly different from what he'd come to know at Grace Fellowship in Savannah. He reminisced for a moment, but the flood of nostalgia was lined with black thoughts. He shook his head, focusing on the tiny words in his Bible. He cleared his throat, looking up. The room was nearly full.

Then the door frame darkened, and all voices stopped. Maxwell stepped inside the sanctuary, white sneakers squeaking against the wood. He nodded to several members of the congregation as he took a seat beside Esther. The two whispered to each other. Maxwell put his arm around the woman, crossed his legs, and looked up at Will, smiling.

Getting the words physically out of his mouth was an even bigger challenge than he'd thought it would be. It was as if his vocal cords had atrophied. But he stuck strictly to scripture for the first several minutes and worked his confidence up enough to chance a peek at the congregation.

He saw that Sally, Frederick, and John had also come in late. They watched Will from the front pew across the aisle from Esther and Maxwell. John looked down at his hands, massaging them nervously. Frederick seemed to stare right through Will, glaring, as if he were focusing not on Will but on the wooden cross which hung behind the pulpit.

"People say that we as individuals are our own worst critics," Will said. "Anybody ever hear that? It means we're harder on ourselves than we are on anybody else. We can't give ourselves a break, because we're always beating ourselves up about the past, or over the latest little insignificant thing in our life. But really, what are these things in the grand scheme?"

The sermon was recycled from his days as a youth pastor, back before he'd been tapped for the senior position at Grace Fellowship. His mind drifted as he preached to the islanders. Thoughts of the past transformed the world around him, shifting the sights, sounds, smells of the present.

Two years back, when West Greene had announced his retirement as pastor at Grace Fellowship, it had come as a shock to all in the congregation except for Will and his wife. The pastor of twenty-four years had felt called into another line of Christian work, and he'd been preparing Will for the transition ever since. God had told West it was time to take his fervor for spreading the gospel to the people. He'd started a street ministry in a poverty-stricken neighborhood on

Savannah's fringes.

During the preceding months, he and Will met twice a week at the old pastor's home for games of one-on-one basketball, followed by tall glasses of ice water and sometimes chocolate-chip cookies. Following that: hours of Bible study in an air-conditioned tool shed—a sort of Christian-themed man cave—behind their suburban Savannah home.

It was during one of these sessions that West told Will his plans to make an announcement at church in which he'd recommend Will, a twenty-eight-year-old seminary-school graduate, as the next senior pastor at Grace Fellowship. As they sat there in the tool shed, the revelation seemed to unravel in slow motion. It meant more to Will than anything in his life. It was a paying gig to supplement his meager landscaping wages, which would help financially. But it was also the realization of a lifelong dream. He'd wanted to be a pastor ever since he was a child, watching West work magic at the pulpit. God really did have a plan, he'd thought. A reason for where we go, where we end up. It was a thought that seemed foolish to him now.

"God gave us this book," Will said, making eye contact with each member of the Muskogee Island congregation. "It's a how-to instruction manual. Complete idiot's guide to living right." A smattering of laughter from the congregation lifted Will's confidence. "Let's turn to Isaiah 43, verse 18."

Nobody moved. It seemed no one in the group had brought a Bible, other than Esther, who flipped carefully through the pages of hers. Maxwell leaned toward her, removing a pair of reading glasses from his shirt pocket.

Will began: "Remember not the former things, neither consider the things of old. Behold, I will do a new thing; now it shall spring forth. I will even make a way in the wilderness, and rivers in the desert, to give drink to my chosen people." He felt his voice growing stronger with the recitation of each gilded word, every anointed syllable. He basked in it.

For the first time since he could remember, Will felt like a man in his element, an artist at work before the canvas. A musician manipulating the strings of an instrument, relishing the sound it makes. It was in these moments of inspiration that Will forgot the past and the future, his mind locking onto the moment. It was for this reason that he noticed too late the symptoms that preceded a seizure.

Sweat formed on his brow, and his face felt clammy. He closed his eyes, lips trembling, stomach turning. He tried to shuffle away from the pulpit, but his legs were bolted to the ground. The feeling died in his appendages.

The next sound that filled the sanctuary was that of paper tearing. The congregation watched, some standing up from their pews, as Will tore pages from his Bible. He ripped the scriptures slowly, wadding the soft paper. The gurgle of maniacal laughter rose in his throat. He dropped the battered tome. Will slumped, hunchbacked, against the pulpit. Teeth snapping together, copper taste on his tongue.

The sanctuary went dark. The hazy light from each of the six windows blinked off one by one. Cold wind kissed his skin. The smells of mildew and old mahogany blew past. His fingers raked splinters from the pulpit, blood streaming from beneath his nails. He felt nothing. Then, silence. Vibration of an alien voice rattled his whole body.

"For the prophet speaks, I will make waste mountains and hills," it growled from somewhere inside him. Will's eardrums throbbed. His chest felt as if it might explode. Hot pain flashed up his sternum. "I will make the rivers islands, and I will dry up the lakes and pools."

His eyes snapped open, and he leveled a frightful gaze at Maxwell Summerour. "I will make the darkness light."

Black and white. Rain patters like prodding fingers against his skull. He sinks. Flashing pain up his neck and spine as salt water fills his mouth, his nose, his lungs. The water feels like fire inside his body, consuming every cell. Snuffing him out. There is no comfort, no warm embrace for this kind of death. Only the torment punching holes. The muffled gurgling of his own voice. There are other voices coming from above. Woeful shouts like delirious laughter. And a hand. Wrinkled bathwater hand of a child reaching down for him.

And then, light.

CHAPTER SIX

Will could hear someone talking as he drifted back toward consciousness. He blinked his eyes, head spinning. Waves of nausea made him cringe. Bitter stomach acid churned its way up his throat. A sharp pain throbbed at the back of his head.

He was indoors, in a dark place. It didn't feel or smell like the sanctuary. There was the faint odor of mildew, but also of mowed grass, wood chips, and mineral spirits. Weak daylight trickled in from somewhere to his right. The room was empty but full of shadows. It seemed he and Maxwell were by themselves.

"Where am I?" Will asked.

Crouched over him, Maxwell smiled. Will groaned, rolling his body to one side, gathering the momentum to sit up on the wooden floor, which was full of splinters. His thoughts were sporadic, unsound, but he remembered something from the sanctuary. The islanders staring at him. Esther standing up, running toward him. And then, nothing.

He could feel the vibration of Maxwell's heavy footfalls on the floor, reverberating through him. He sat up, taking stock of the room. Sharp objects and rusted mechanisms hung from the walls, suspended by single nails driven into the lumber. The wood was in an early phase of rotting, black mold spreading across the surface.

"I came here two years ago," Maxwell said, his voice seeming to come from all around the dark room as if through stereo speakers in an auditorium. "You should have seen the state of things. It would have made you sick. The laziness. I just couldn't believe how preposterous the whole thing was. Here they are, these artists, writers or whatever. All they do is complain when they don't have the time to practice their craft, because they're busy with whatever it is they do, which I assure you is absolutely fucking nothing. And they're right here in paradise." Maxwell stuffed his hands in his pockets, pacing. "You give something good to people like this, and it means nothing. I despise nothing else in this world more than entitlement."

Will pushed up from the floor, standing on wobbly legs. His mind raced. How had he ended up in this strange room with Maxwell? He looked around, spotting the source of meager light: a window with blinds over it, late afternoon sun filtering through it. "How long was I out?" he asked.

Maxwell stopped pacing. He pulled a flask from his back pocket and took a long swig, swishing the liquid around in his mouth. "The things I've done for these people," Maxwell said. "It would amaze you. Do you know that when I came here there was no fertile ground? The fields, these glorious fields that had flourished for years, they were overrun with briars and saplings. The only fruit you could find was blackberries, and that was only from sheer neglect. And where do you think these artists had been getting their food before I arrived?" He stared, awaiting an answer.

"They had it shipped in?" Will said.

Maxwell nodded, frowning. "I've restored a natural order here, Will. Do you see that?"

Feeling queasy, Will placed hands on his knees for support. "Can we open a window?"

Maxwell pulled open blinds and shoved a window open. Will walked over, leaning heavily against the screen. They were in a building surrounded by woods. He saw the back of the plantation in the distance and realized they were inside the old tool shed.

"I find myself out here sometimes," said Maxwell. "Reminds me of my childhood. My mother raised me by herself. She worked hard. She was the maid for a very wealthy Savannah businessman. We lived in a shack on the far end of this rich man's property. We had a mattress and a chest of drawers we shared. A wooden box where we kept our canned food. There was a water faucet out back we used for bathing. But we weren't allowed to use the bathrooms in the mansion. That was off-limits.

"I spent day after day in that old shack," Maxwell continued. "During the summers when school was out, I got to actually go inside and help my mother clean. The things I saw, they fascinated me. The way these people lived. Their refrigerator and cabinets full of food. I couldn't believe it. I'd walk through the house, from one huge room to another, pretending I was some kind of king.

"I got in trouble once for eating out of the trash can. Their brat son had eaten the middle out of a bologna sandwich and just thrown the rest away. This man—the wealthy businessman my mother worked for—he happened to walk into the kitchen and he found me digging through the garbage, chewing on the crust.

"Maybe that's why I grew up wanting to be rich. I was obsessed with it when I was a kid. I wanted to be able to enjoy these things I'd never known." Maxwell ran his fingers along the bent teeth of a rusty saw. "What about you, Will? Was your youth privileged?"

Will shook his head. His family, too, had struggled financially. Following the accidental death of Will's father, they'd been forced to sell their home in suburban Savannah. His mother worked nights at McDonald's. During the day she drove a truck, filling breakroom vending machines all over Savannah with prepackaged subs, sausage biscuits, and microwaveable cups of soup. She stacked food in the buzzing, refrigerator-sized machines and removed the expired products. Whenever she could, Callie Fordham stowed outdated bags of salt-and-vinegar chips and chicken-salad sandwiches in her purse. Returning home to their two-room apartment, she'd dump the contents on the kitchen table. More often than not, it was their dinner.

Getting by without Will's father proved very difficult. The funeral costs alone had set them back drastically. It would darken the days for Callie as she struggled to make ends meet. She openly cursed her dead husband for not having life insurance. She wept bitterly in bed at night. Will could hear her sobbing through the walls.

He'd lie awake too, thinking about his father's final fateful moments in the backyard, sprawled on his back, staring into the storm clouds. Jack Fordham's eyes had been wide with disbelief as he clutched absently at the big tarp, his fingers squeezing at the blue blanket of polyethylene. It made crunching noises, flagging in the wind like a superhero's cape. He'd held onto it all the way down. Will had watched his father countless times move with great ease along the steep grade of their roof, securing tarps before a storm. He'd done it a hundred times to keep the rain from invading their home. It seemed impossible that he'd actually made a mistake.

But he had. Jack Fordham's shoe slipped on the tarp, and he fell nearly thirty feet, taking a length of the gutter spout down with him. When the ambulance arrived, there was nothing they could do.

⟲

For a very long time, Will carried his grief with him wherever he went. He tallied the days that followed the death of his father, hoping the distance in time would provide some solace. It did not. He mentally withdrew at school, compounding the problems he was already having in class. They thought he was stupid. Teachers sent home letters that his mom never saw. The principal once left a message on their phone at the apartment, though Will managed to delete it before Callie could hear it.

One day, Will's fifth-grade teacher told him to stay after class. That afternoon, he sat across from the woman at her desk. Nervously, she told him that he was being transferred to another classroom. He would have a different teacher from here on out. She called it a "special classroom" for "special students." The ticking clock on the wall seemed absurdly loud in the quiet room. Every time the teacher said the word "special," her eyes would dart, finding the face of the noisy clock. "Do you understand what I'm saying, Will?"

He nodded, and the gesture sealed his fate for the rest of his days in the Savannah-Chatham County Public School System. He hadn't blamed the woman for her decision. By all appearances, it seemed something was in fact mentally wrong with him. He had not yet learned to silence the waves of panic that crept into his thoughts, discovered how to ignore the mind pictures or the noises. Often, he'd find himself stopped in the middle of school hallways, staring off into space while classmates fanned out around him, laughing. The lucid

65

glimpses often came when he least expected them, and the clarity was jarring. He could see sentient shadows spreading in the spaces above the school building's ceiling tiles, among the support beams and pink insulation. Black masses with long human fingers stretched out in the storage rooms and janitor's closets, making high-pitched noises at one another.

Will wasn't the only one who saw these things. In ninth grade, he shared a classroom with a group of young people who had varying degrees of mental and physical disabilities, autism, and behavioral disorders. The varsity softball coach oversaw the students and their learning endeavors. For class lessons, he handed out phone books for them to thumb through. He wheeled a big television out of an adjacent closet and turned on Saturday-morning cartoons that he recorded each weekend on a VHS tape.

A sixteen-year-old boy with severe autism named Rocky used to shriek whenever "Coach" would open the closet door. His hand would go to his mouth, and sometimes he would bawl and hyperventilate until the door was shut. Rocky liked Will. He complained when Will wasn't there. He'd chirp with great enthusiasm, pointing to the air above Will as if a butterfly were about to land, often stirring the class into a frenzy. Sometimes Rocky would turn to Will in the middle of class, regarding him with a knowing smile.

Ninth grade was the same year Will had his first seizure. It happened on a Sunday.

At fourteen years old, he was a regular at Grace Fellowship, hitching a ride aboard the church bus that arrived at his apartment complex once a week. At church, he often felt the mental tension melt away. Sitting in the sanctuary singing hymns, it was as if someone had turned off the radio tuner in his brain. In the sanctuary, he got a unique feeling: the sensation of being somewhere he belonged.

He became a regular on Sundays, often staying afterward to help clean up. When the congregation was gone, it was just him and Pastor West. There was something good in the man's heart, Will realized. He could sense it. Will swept and vacuumed the floors while West went from bathroom to bathroom, scrubbing the toilets and refilling the hand sanitizer. Because the man lived fairly close to Will's apartment complex, he took the boy home most afternoons.

One afternoon, West locked up the building and walked out to his car expecting to see Will there. But he was not. West set his Bible and notebook down in the driver's seat and shut the door. He called out, but got no response. He made his way around the chapel, peering around the corners. He unlocked the doors of the church and called out to an empty sanctuary.

He walked the grounds and had all but given up, when he saw something out the corner of his eye. There was a flash of fabric in the grass, billowing between two headstones in the church cemetery. Among the clover and crabgrass, Will lay flat against the ground, red ants climbing all over his body. His expression was that of someone who had just seen a ghost. West extended an arm and pulled him up.

The world had a name for Will's condition: epilepsy. But the visions were harder to explain. He'd always had them, but never so vivid as in the moments before a seizure. Whatever Will had seen before losing consciousness that afternoon was hazy. Short-term memory loss often accompanied seizures, a fact he would come to know later in life. But if he thought about it hard enough, he remembered seeing a machine in the sky.

It was enormous, shapeless, and monstrous. It was grotesque. Encased in a see-through skin, its insides were a puzzle of bones and rust. Plungers and springs pumped liquid through scabbed-over valves. Thick discharge dripped from membranous, metallic ribs. A sea of cilia propelled it through the clouds as the gears churned, slick with human blood.

⬯

"I need some air," Will said, his head beginning to clear. He stumbled toward the door, exiting the shed. The fresh air was intoxicating. He gorged himself on it, taking great gulps.

Maxwell followed him, shutting the door. It was early evening. The air felt cool as the sun descended, casting shadows in the wooded area where they stood. Will looked toward the plantation home, eyeing an expansive cornfield between them and the house. The rows of withered stalks glowed a golden hue in the early autumn light.

"We've worked hard to make that corn flourish. Too bad you couldn't see it before the harvest," Maxwell said. "Beautiful. There's no more left now except the leftovers we use to make mash. You ever seen a real moonshine still?"

They walked a path behind the shed. At the end of the trail, there were two copper cylinders, each balanced on a knee-high pile of flat rocks. A single pipe connected the cylinders, and a second pipe descended from the middle barrel, where it was coiled like a rattlesnake atop another pile of rocks. Below the coiled piping was a small barrel to collect the condensed vapors. Feeling the tug of old habits, Will reflexively leaned over the barrel, peering inside.

"None in there," Maxwell laughed. "But I'll take care of us." He stepped behind the trunk of an oak tree, removing a ceramic jug from behind it. He uncorked it, offering Will the first pull. Will took the container, feeling it cold and smooth against his rough hands. Everything inside him screamed to put it down. This was the wrong path. *If you do this, there is nothing different from the place you left. The act of transition has meant nothing, and you are weak.* His hands tilted the jug to his lips in a swift motion, as if his thirst were sentient. Warmth flooded his body, spreading through his arms, legs, and fingertips. For a fleeting moment, he forgot everything about the past. He felt whole. Tipping it up again, he swallowed more.

"There you go, son," Maxwell said, taking the jug. He then turned it up for several seconds, his Adam's apple bobbing beneath wrinkled skin. "Let's just both relax a little. I want you to take it easy. No more of this Holy Roller nonsense."

"What do you mean?"

"When you were up there at the pulpit today, I could have sworn I was looking at a different man. Not the meek pastor. You scared that boy, you know. Poor John didn't know what was going on."

"It was a seizure. I can't help what happens."

Maxwell shook his head. "Some people might have found what you did inspirational. Many on this island are easily swayed. They have weak minds. They'll mistake your ailments for spiritual conviction. Let's try and keep the sermons tame from here on out. I'm not one to micromanage, but I brought you here for a reason. Frightening the people of Muskogee wasn't part of the deal."

Will took the jug back from Maxwell, taking a sip.

Maxwell placed a hand on Will's shoulder. "I think we've got a lot in common, Will, even more than our humble beginnings. You consider yourself a man of God, maybe even a prophet. I'm here as a prophet too. I have visions. A time of great transition is coming, and you're going to play a big part."

CHAPTER SEVEN

The next day, Will found John in the commons area, a dusty clearing centrally located among the old slave cabins. Throughout
the day, artists crisscrossed the grounds toting produce, water, and—
when they were productive—artwork to show one another. Sometimes
a Muskogee hog came nosing along to forage for what the islanders
had dropped beneath the picnic tables. Much like the cabins, the picnic tables were made of sand, oyster, and limestone. Will found them
sturdy, but not much in the way of comfort.

As he approached, he saw John seated at one of the tables with
the fat man the islanders called the Teacher. The man smirked as John
stared at the chessboard between them. They had just begun a new
game. The black and white pieces were still separate, although a renegade black rook and the white queen had ventured into enemy territory.

"Not gonna work," the Teacher said with a chuckle. "But I see
what you're doing here, John. I like it. It's very good, actually."

Will stayed put, watching them for several minutes. John was facing in the opposite direction, so he had not seen him approach.

"You play?" asked a female voice. Will turned. It was the darkly
tanned woman with the facial scar. She was hard at work cleaning a

potter's kick wheel, scraping away dried mud.

"It's been a while. You?"

"The Teacher's always looking for an opponent, and sometimes I let him win," she said, furrowing her brow as she leaned against the table scrubbing, forearms bulging.

"I'm Will."

"I know who you are," she said.

"You need a hand with that?"

"Oh, no. You start cleaning up after these people, you'll put me out of a job."

"You're not an artist?"

"Me? I can't even draw a stick figure." Wiping hands on the front of her shirt, she outstretched a hand. "Brandi."

Her grip was firm, her palm calloused. She offered a smile, but her green eyes bore some kind of sadness. "You're pretty good-looking for a pastor."

Reaching into her back pocket, she produced a metal putty knife and resumed work on the potter's kick wheel, scraping a stubborn clump of hardened clay from the apparatus. She leaned over the table, and the loose collar of her ragged T-shirt fell open.

She looked up at him, seemingly aware of what she was doing. "Did you hurt your head at the church?" she asked.

He averted his eyes. "I'm fine. It was nothing."

"You hit the floor pretty hard."

"Yes, I'm better."

"I'll tell you what," she said. "Pastor Argus did some pretty crazy stuff. He spoke in tongues and ran around in circles. Got on all fours and barked like a dog. But you really had me convinced. Now, I don't believe in the Holy Ghost, but if I ever got saved, you'd be the one to convince me. How did you do that thing with your voice?"

Will felt a tug at his shirt. John stood beside him clutching a backpack, a notebook, and his pair of binoculars.

"Did you win?" Will asked him.

"The boy is talented," the Teacher interrupted, calling out from the picnic table. He shook his head as he folded up the chessboard. "He's a quiet one, but there's a lot going on in that brain."

⎯

They set out on the swamp with a canteen full of water and some leftover bacon and pancakes in a ziplock bag. The vessel was a rusted jon boat with two seats and plastic oars that seemed more appropriate for a kayak. It cut through the green surface of algae skin with ease. Will rowed. John perched on the edge of his seat, binoculars in hand.

In addition to the boat, which was equipped with special handles for a handicapped person, they had two fishing poles with rusty spinner bait tied to ten-pound test line. "Are there really fish in here?" Will asked. "Looks pretty gross."

The boy removed the binoculars, letting them fall against his chest. "My dad caught a big fish in here," he said, holding his hands two feet apart. "This big."

Relying on John's memory, they rowed toward a stranded piece of land out on the swamp. An island on an island, John had called it. He had once visited there with his father, he explained. He'd described it to Will as if it were some secret, foreign jungle. He had not been there since his father took him, and that was more than three years ago. "We'll be there in less than ten minutes," John said.

It was a breath of fresh air spending time alone with the boy.

John rattled off facts about native birds and scribbled in his notebook. Sometimes he'd hop up from his perch, excited at the prospect of a new sighting. Or he'd drop the binoculars, turning his head to listen to an unusual chirp or shriek. "Did you hear that? Warbler? No, no. Chuck-will's-widow."

Will felt lost in the moment, and he was very happy. Out on the water with John, he was reminded of the way time would stretch out so unusually when he used to play games with Aaron. That was one of the perks of spending time with kids. On your own, you got so stuck in your head, drowning in the day's worries, to-do lists, and planning. Always planning. You could truly lose yourself, though, in the unbridled excitement of a child. You could live vicariously in the unburdened ecstasy of adolescence, and Will missed that so much.

But John wasn't exactly unburdened, was he? Recalling the boy's disturbing words from several nights ago, Will let his curiosity get the better of him. He could have let it be. He could have let this moment coast on for just a little longer. Instead, he pried.

"Tell me about Pastor Argus. What happened to him?"

John picked up one of the fishing poles. He plucked the spinner-bait's rusty treble hook from one of the eyelets, letting it dangle in the air before casting it toward open water. It hit the swamp with a soft splash, sinking into the muck. John reeled it in too swiftly. The line respooled in a bird's nest, too tangled to cast again. "Dang it," the boy muttered. "Stupid."

"Let me see it," Will said. He took it, examining the rod and reel. He released the line slowly, inch by inch, threading it back out between thumb and forefinger.

"Everybody keeps saying Pastor Argus died of natural causes. That's what Sall—my mom keeps saying. 'Natural causes.' But I was up on the cliff. That place I showed you. He was down there next to the Crescent. He was screaming at God. He kept screaming so loud. I wanted to go down and help him. It looked like he was tied to the rocks. Frederick was down there, just watching him scream. I would have helped him if I could. I liked him. Pastor Argus was nice to me. I didn't know what to do."

Will finished untangling the line and handed John the fishing pole. It was such an insane story. He didn't know what to think. Who would do something like that to a nice, old pastor, and why? It didn't make any sense. "Are you sure?"

"You don't believe me."

"I didn't say that."

"Well, I haven't told anybody else about it."

"Why not?"

"Because Sally was down there too," John said. "And Maxwell. They were just standing there watching. The tide was coming up. The waves were crashing on his head, and then Pastor Argus just stopped moving."

There was a sudden spray of water beside the boat. The dark swish of a large, scaly tail whipped the surface. The animal disappeared before they'd gotten a good glimpse, but it looked very big. Will watched as a shadow vanished beneath the murk. John shrugged, as if to say, *I never said there wouldn't be alligators.*

"I think they did the same thing to my dad that they did to Pastor Argus," John said. "I think Sally and Maxwell planned it."

"What? How would your dad even get out in the ocean if he was . . . if he was in the wheelchair? And why do you keep calling her Sally?"

"My real mom died when I was two. Sally's my dad's second wife. She hates me."

"Why do you say that?" Will asked, although he had indeed sensed resentment.

John took the canteen out of his backpack. Taking a sip, he offered it to Will. He took the metal canister from John and unscrewed the top.

"See those trees coming up out of the water?" John said. "Just past those. There's a dry place we can pull up."

———

They gazed at the dome-like canopy of foliage above. Neither breathed a word as birds chattered and whistled, a chorus of locusts clacked and buzzed, and a nearby frog uttered a solemn belch. It felt as if they had indeed entered another land far from Muskogee Island. The trees towered above them, Spanish moss spilling from the branches, weakening the harsh midday sun.

"Told you it was amazing," John said.

They crunched across fallen palm fronds, cutting a straight path through an open circle of land where no trees grew. Will asked John what kept trees from flourishing in this spot.

"What do you *think*?" John said. "Alligators. This is an alligator den."

Will tried to picture himself and the boy fleeing giant reptiles. He struggled to remember what he'd once read about escaping alligators. Run in a zigzag pattern? It seemed crazy that something like that would really work. "Don't worry," John said as if sensing Will's uneasiness. "I'll protect us." He pulled the lock blade out of his pocket. Flicking it open, he waved it threateningly at an invisible foe. He brought the knife down in a stabbing motion, sinking it into the ground.

They stopped for lunch beside a big oak tree. They nibbled at dry pancakes and bacon. Then they sat in silence for nearly half an hour, listening to the island noises and passing the canteen back and forth. John stood up and said he had to go to the bathroom. Will told him to be careful. He felt sleepy and could feel himself nodding off. He wanted to stay here forever with the boy. The idea of going back to Maxwell, Sally, Frederick, and the others made him uneasy.

Staring up at the trees, he slid down to a reclining position and dozed. He awoke once, glancing around for John. The sounds of the island were soothing: chirping birds and buzzing bugs. He gazed up at the trees, drooping with the scaly stems of Spanish moss. He'd read once that the epiphytic plants were not parasites but could damage tree limbs with their weight. The thoughts swirled in his mind, and he slipped into a half sleep.

In his dream, the Spanish moss came to life. It dripped down from tree branches. Mounds of the stuff scooted along the ground like sentient gray wigs. Each clump crawled toward a larger clump of moss, congregating. It writhed, growing larger in the dirt just a few feet away from Will. Out of the mass, a figure began to form: the vague silhouette of a human being with unnaturally long arms and legs. A long neck stretched up as tall as the branches. It twisted toward Will: a face with no eyes, nose, or ears. A large mouth opened in a horrid smile. The smell of rotten wood and bug excrement enveloped him. He awoke, gasping.

There was a crackling in the underbrush. He thought at first that he'd dragged some dream remnant into waking life. He stood, walking around the tree trunk. He called out for John. There was no answer.

A small yaupon holly bush swayed with recent motion. Its bright red berries bobbed. This was the native plant used to make black drink. Days earlier, he'd seen Sally outside one of the slave cabins, stripping the branches clean of the bulbous, toxic berries. She pruned the branches down to small clusters before placing them on a blackened baking sheet. Once cooked, the twigs and leaves were crumbled into a bubbling cauldron over the fire. The same potion used by the Native Americans on Muskogee Island for thousands of years was the beverage of choice for these "spoiled rich kids," as Maxwell had called them.

The desire to connect with nature and channel some spirit of artistic inspiration was rooted in a tradition so old nobody could understand it. The painting in the plantation house showed the island's original inhabitants swilling from cups on the beach. A religious rite of passage, it was meant to bring them closer to God. Like the peyote-eating Indians of another region, they used a substance to induce hallucinations. They drank black drink until they would vomit—it was a purging of the flesh and an opening of the soul. Will had gleaned as much from Howard Mansell's notes, anyway.

Despite the historical prevalence of the yaupon holly on Muskogee, he'd not seen much of the plant until just now. The tree-like bush likely suffered the same fate as much of the other flora here—choked to death by wisteria. It wouldn't be long until wisteria smothered every other plant on the island.

"John," Will called out, peering into the forest. He'd been gone too long. It was early afternoon now, the sun beating down on the back of his neck. Pushing away the pointy palmettos, he walked deeper into the woods. A bird exploded from the underbrush, screeching. He watched it escape into the sky, a flash of white and yellow.

"Boo!"

Will jumped.

John was in hysterics. "You thought I was an alligator, didn't you?"

⌒

Once John was settled on his side of the boat, Will pushed off with a running start, then climbed onto his seat, placing the plastic oars in the holsters. He fell into the rhythm of rowing.

He watched John. The boy was so fascinated with the natural world. The binoculars rarely left his eyes, except when he scribbled notes. His head darted this way and that, scanning the waters and land.

"What is it about birds?" Will asked.

John shrugged.

"My son used to like birds."

"What's his name?" said John.

"Aaron."

"Where is he?"

Will slowed the rhythm of the oars without realizing it.

John nodded. "He died."

Will let the silence answer.

"Do you still think about him?"

"Every day."

"I don't ever stop thinking about my dad. I think good people go to heaven when they die. One day, God's going to get revenge on the bad people for what they did." John scanned the waters. "They don't know that I know about Pastor Argus, or they'd kill me too."

"Nobody's going to hurt you," Will said. "You're just a kid."

"Yes, they will. I saw something I wasn't supposed to."

Will stopped rowing, setting the plastic oars down. He and John rocked gently in the vessel as the water slapped lightly against the metal.

79

"What if I could prove to you that nobody got murdered? Would you stop worrying then?"

"How are you going to do that? I know what I saw."

"I could ask around."

"No! Maxwell and Frederick, they'll find out. They'll come for me."

John was right. Will couldn't breathe a word of any of this. Not that he for one second believed what he was hearing, but what if by some stretch there really was something to it? It wasn't worth putting John in danger to try and prove a point.

"Okay. What if I do some digging around?"

"Yeah! We could do it together. We could sneak back into the plantation house. Maxwell's got more stuff hidden in his bedroom. More secrets."

"That's where you found the box with your dad's stuff?"

"Yes."

"We can't just go breaking into people's houses," Will said. "But let me do some looking around. If I see anything that gives me any reason to think you're not safe here, you and me, we'll leave, okay? We'll get on a boat and go."

"Just make sure nobody follows you." John said, reaching for the oars. He and Will switched places. Will examined the world through John's binoculars, while John rowed them back to the main land. This is crazy, Will thought.

―◯―

Once they'd returned, and he and John parted ways, Will made his way toward the cabin. It was midafternoon, the sun casting long silhouettes between tree trunks. The woods were quieter than usual, he thought, as he hiked down the path. There was something about total silence in the woods that felt unnatural. He stopped and listened. There was only the sound of his own breathing. The trail disappeared up ahead, winding its way around a corner. Dark-colored branches drooped low over the path. The dense foliage was made up of both bright and dark green, splashes of color amid an otherwise ominous-feeling landscape.

A diseased oak tree caught his eye. Black tumors as big as golf balls blistered its limbs, burdening the branches with excess weight. It bent toward the trail like a tired traveler. Its affliction was caused by tiny insects called black oak gall wasps. Will had researched the symptoms once while helping a landscaping client whose prized oak tree had been stricken. The only way to cure it had been with chemicals. Here on Muskogee, there was no hope for this young tree, he thought, running fingers along the bulbous swellings.

Cold wind blew through the branches, a sudden gale that sent a chill up his spine. All at once, he got the sensation that someone or something was standing—or crouching—behind him. Not hiding in the trees. Not somewhere else far down the trail. But nearby, close enough to breathe on him.

He turned slowly, and he saw the shadows.

They moved about in the trees, lanky apparitions with freakish bodies. Long human fingers wrapped around the trunks. Hollow-eyed devils, peering at him. They scaled the branches. They moved from plant to plant. Their insect-like wings made a crackling sound as they rubbed against one another. They were the same as those he'd seen so long ago in the rafters and closets of his high school. They'd followed him here. There was no escape.

But it's not real, he thought. Your mind is sick. It's the same as with the machines in the sky. All this time in church, trying to interpret the visions, the reasons for all of this. He should have visited a psychiatrist. He'd made the basic mistake of placing meaning behind what was nothing more than a disease of the mind. He continued walking, willing the demons to disappear one by one.

Arriving at the cabin, he placed John's binoculars on the nightstand. He'd forgotten to return them to the boy. He collapsed on the bed. Closing his eyes, he struggled to clear his mind of the unreality of his visions. He attempted to make sense of the boy's paranoia. None of it seemed to compute. Maybe there was something Will was missing. Why would someone hurt, much less murder, an old pastor? Was Pastor Argus crazy? Maybe. But that's no reason to kill a guy. And the idea that somebody had killed John's dad too? Insane. What would somebody stand to gain? The kid had to be suffering from delusions. Or maybe he was just that desperate for attention from the newcomer, likely the only fresh face he'd seen in years.

From under his bed, he dug out the Tupperware container John had given him. He opened it, shuffling through the old news clippings. He took his time reading a couple of the columns. One of the articles was about the eminent domain issue with Esther and Arch Holdings, another was a personality profile on Pastor Argus. The final column he read delved into the mystery of the Crescent, pondering how it came to be.

Placing the binoculars inside the Tupperware container, Will snapped the lid shut and slid it back under the bed. He shut his eyes, breathing deeply, and drifted in and out of sleep for about an hour. He dreamed about his past life. He walked through the backyard with Rose and Aaron. They had a water balloon fight. As quickly as Will could fill the balloons, his three-year-old son would bust them, laughing. He awoke dripping with sweat. He got out of bed and left the cabin.

◯

The sun was setting as he approached the Crescent.

Will took off his shoes, feeling the cool sand beneath his feet. The all-day burn of the island sun was gone now. The early autumn wind picked up, whipping his hair. He eyed the monolithic silhouettes on the beach ahead. The large tide pool just past the stones rippled with the gale. Its surface reflected clouds in the sky, smeared thumbprints of gray on a filthy canvas. Ghost crabs raced across the beach, crisscrossing one another, diving in and popping out of burrows. A lone seagull paced the shoreline, prodding clumps of kelp with its beak. The bird took flight as Will came closer, walking toward the nine stone benches.

What struck him was the color. Each bench was an otherworldly greenish blue. Swirls of translucent grains ran up and down the length of each slab. Will trailed his fingertips across the back of one of the benches. It was cold and rough. On the middle bench was a half circle of burned-out candle stubs, melted wax puddling atop the stone surface. He eyed the blackened remnants of an old campfire in the center of the Crescent, charred hunks of driftwood scattered in the ash. Beside the fire pit was a well-used roasting pan. For cooking the tea leaves, he figured.

He looked out toward the ocean, and a weak splashing in the tide pool caught his eye. It was low tide, and there was a fish trapped in the waters. He walked toward the tide pool. The fish broke the surface again. Its spiny dorsal fin and the black spots on its tail were the give-

83

away: It was a medium-sized red drum. As it continued to writhe in the shallows, Will rolled up the legs of his jeans and stepped into the tide pool. Careful to avoid the sharp spines on the front fin, he grabbed the fish by the mouth. It squirmed as he lifted it and carried it to the ocean. Standing ankle-deep in the waves, he released the red drum. It wiggled from his grasp, disappearing in the surf. Will turned around and headed back, the tide sucking out the sand beneath his feet.

He stopped at the tide pool.

There were four unusual-looking holes in the wet sand. Spaced evenly apart, the sunken spots made up a sort of rectangle on the ocean side of the tide pool, just a few yards away from the Crescent. He kicked at the sand around one of the pits. There was something shiny inside. Will squatted, scooping sediment out of the hole to find a big stone buried at the bottom. He tried to clear all the sand away from it, but the stone was too large. He stood up, crossing his arms.

Will examined the next hollow in the ground. Getting down on his hands and knees, he dug out the sand. Another large rock. There seemed to be four big rocks buried in the sand about six feet apart from each other. The width of a man's armspan. The length of a man lying down. A chill ran up his spine as he recalled John's description of Argus Greene's final moments. The old pastor tied to rocks and thrashing in the surf. He tried to remember what else the boy had said.

This was the secluded beach. The one nobody comes to. *It's off-limits.*

Will turned, looking toward the precipice where he had stood with the boy just a few nights earlier. He saw someone. It was too far off to make out who it was, but somebody was there. The person lingered for a moment, staring down toward Will. It wasn't John. It was an adult. Will started toward the precipice for a better look.

The person shrank away, disappearing from his sight.

The following are selections from "Eyes on the Island," a weekly column by deceased Savannah *Daily Post* columnist Howard Mansell.

April 2, 2008

Why I Moved to Muskogee

When cut off from the world—from the luxury of cell phones, cable television, and the endorphin drips of our digital realm—your mind begins to wander. You think about your place in society. You think about the things you didn't think about while gazing at your computer screen.

When somebody goes off the grid, or disconnects, he or she does so at the risk of self-imposed ostracism from a world that doesn't have patience for those who lag behind. Those who walk out of step. For this reason alone, I got many a wayward glance when I told colleagues my plans to move out to Muskogee.

Some were shocked at the very prospect of a life without readily available electricity and hot showers. Their jaws dropped when they learned I was going to be living in an artist colony. The notion that this forward-thinking, scientific-minded journalist who dwells only in the realm of fact was going to reside in a den of kooks gone native—it didn't sit right with everyone.

Well, as to the lack of electricity. I can tell you in all honesty that I don't miss it. The hot showers? Yep, I miss those. And as far as this colony full of artsy types, with their drum circles, herbal tea, and plans to save us all from corporate greed, well, you're talking about my wife now, so cut it out.

Sally was indeed the driving force in winning me over to this wild idea, and for this I am eternally grateful to her. Life on Muskogee has caused me to discover things about myself and about my relation to the natural world that I could never have gleaned from books.

As I write this now, I'm sitting before a natural vista with a pristine view of the oceanfront. It's God's country, and in God's country, one must be reverent. And so I sit and listen to the island birds, and I hear the sound of the surf whooshing back and forth, and I feel I am a part of this place. My four-year-old son, John, is here with me, and he is silent as well, taking in this moment of tranquility, the significance of which he too can sense.

It's a feeling of camaraderie with something bigger than yourself. One cannot come close to such convictions when one is distant from the beating heart of nature. It's for this reason that human beings, despite living right on top of one another in crowded cities, are apt to feel a sense of isolation.

If we stop, look, and listen to the natural beauty all around us, it becomes astonishingly clear that we are not alone on this earth. Out on the quiet island of Muskogee, I've found a perfect society that wants for nothing. All that separates you, loyal reader, from yours truly is a half dozen miles of salt water. But you should see the difference it can make on a man's mind.

August 7, 2008

Argus in the Throes of the Holy Ghost

When Pastor Argus Greene invokes the Holy Ghost, his hands begin to tremble. For the congregation inside Muskogee Chapel, it's not hard to see the tremors that quake the pulpit, the feverish look in the old man's eyes as he lapses into a delirium, shouting in strange tongues.

Anything can happen.

This past Sunday, Pastor Greene stepped off the stage, took a deep breath, and sprinted down the aisles, past the pews, and out the door—all the while screaming at the top of his lungs.

Several weeks back, he stopped in the middle of his sermon, scratched his head, and removed a ballpoint pen from his shirt pocket. He approached the wall of the sanctuary, and he started drawing pictures of boats and fish.

It's gotten to the point that many in the artist colony come to church just to see what the old man will do. But Pastor Greene is more than a Holy Roller. Though he suffers from what a doctor might deem Alzheimer's, the man is actually quite interesting. Even more interesting? His family history.

There is written and geologic evidence of a "Great Flood" here on Muskogee in the mid to late 1800s. What was likely an enormous tropical storm struck the island one day without warning, killing rich Spanish landowners and countless slaves.

As the story goes, the ancestors of Argus Greene were prepared for the rising waters. Months before the flood, God had spoken to Lunsford Greene, a man many people thought insane. "Build a raft," the voices had told him. When the waves crashed down on Muskogee, Lunsford and his wife climbed to the top of their cabin, where they untethered a massive raft that the man had built. They stayed afloat as the waters rose, riding out the sudden storm surge. And they survived. Greene buried the island's dead and lived for two more decades, fathering several children.

It's said that mental illness can run in the family. But prophecy?

My young son does his best to suppress laughter when Pastor Greene stops his sermon, dancing a jig across the stage. The adults here on Muskogee do much the same, only they hide their laughter a little better. As we sit in the pews, watching the old man's hands tremble, hearing him shout in strange tongues, I often wonder if maybe we shouldn't pay a little closer attention to what he says. It's hurricane season.

December 12, 2010

Don't Gamble with Paradise

I'm doing something a little unusual this week. I'm dedicating the space I'm allotted for my column to voice a plea to the officials of the Port of Savannah: Do not use eminent domain to steal what is not yours. Chairman Gundermann: I know times are tough. I know that money talks. I know the prospect of generating tax dollars is an appealing notion in these times of financial strain. But I urge you to look at the big picture.

Financial recovery will come. Already, there are signs of an economic boom in the Port of Savannah. The Associated Press reported two weeks back that our coastal seaports are on track to finish fiscal year 2010 with record cargo volumes. The Georgia Ports Authority handled 23.8 million tons of imports and exports during the first six months of the year. That's 12 percent growth over the previous fiscal year. Things are looking up. So why now should you consider that obscene notion of eminent domain?

Arch Holdings brought their offer to the table last week in a gift-wrapped package with a nice, shiny bow. The steel company's owner, Alex Thigpen, presented a benefits package to the Port of Savannah that promised a 2 percent increase in tax revenue. It seems the import and export of steel products will fetch a great fortune for not only the proprietors of Arch Holdings but the Port itself.

And now we hear rumblings of the eminent domain.

Muskogee Island belongs to Esther Campbell. Politicians, you may have found a loophole, but right is right. Wrong is wrong. I ask you, Chairman Gundermann, to consider how it might look to take this island from an elderly woman and then sell it to a company that will strip it clean and line their pockets with profit.

For those reading this, here's a little civics lesson about eminent domain: It is the right of a government to expropriate private property for public use with payment of compensation.

Is it legal? Unfortunately, yes.

In my time as a government reporter, I've seen politicians do far worse. Be watchful, fellow citizens, because there are those among us who revere only the Almighty Dollar. The rape and destruction of Muskogee Island is a means to attain further riches for Arch Holdings. It is our duty to make sure these businessmen do not find their way through the loopholes. And it's on you, Chairman Gundermann, to guard Muskogee Island from such demise.

January 28, 2011

The 'Eye of God' Watches Us

One of the lesser-known but more mysterious features here on Muskogee is a monument on the island's southeast corner. It's assumed to have been built by the Creek Indians centuries and centuries ago. The curiosity is made up of nine large stones arranged in a half circle on the beach. A circular tide pool at its base fills with water as the moon's gravity tugs on the Atlantic.

People on the island call it "the Crescent." Located on a small strip of beach on a somewhat secluded area of the Muskogee coast, the nine rocks serve as benches where a select few members of the artist colony sometimes gather. But this group of artistically inclined islanders wasn't the first to have this idea. It's thought to have been a sacred and ancient gathering place for Muskogee's original inhabitants.

Through mail correspondence with the Society for Creek Culture, I've discovered that the Crescent is a religious monument built as tribute to a native god: Esaugetuh Emissee ("Master of Breath"). The native people believed that the entire world was once all underwater. The so-called Master of Breath created humanity from a mound of clay on a hill.

My contact with the Society for Creek Culture said the shape of this landmark is also identical to a symbol found on ancient artwork from centuries back. The open-ended circle is a recurring pattern known as the "Eye of God."

The society's spokesman said that only the leaders of a Muskogee tribe would have been granted admission into the circle.

Inside our island's plantation, a painting hangs above the kitchen doorway that depicts a group of dark-colored men sitting in the half circle. They share a beverage together, while a wild-eyed man dances before them. The moon glows brightly above the group. There's no date on the painting, and it's too worn by time to read the name of the painter.

The mystery is this: How did the rocks get here? They are greenish blue and are of a cloudy variety of quartzite usually found in the Blue Ridge or Piedmont regions of Georgia. For such rocks to end up here is nothing short of miraculous. Just ask any geologist, and you'll get an incredulous look. The stones don't belong here, and nobody knows how they got here.

But the Crescent is an inseparable and essential monument of Muskogee Island. As I watch members of the artist colony seated on the stones eating their meals, making jokes, trimming their toenails, and making light of what these monoliths represent, I can't help but wonder if there's some all-seeing deity—a Master of Breath, if you will—watching it all with a furrowed brow: the sacred half circle defiled by intruders.

HIGH TIDE

CHAPTER EIGHT

Will and Sally stood chest deep in the calm surf as the sun crept over the horizon. She took his hand, threading her fingers between his, and pulled him deeper into the water. He hesitated. Her hand traced a line down his back. Pulling him closer, she looked him in the eyes. "I want you to stay here," she said. "You're home now."

It had been more than two weeks since his trip down to the Crescent, and ever since, Sally had been coming on to him more often. She'd sometimes show up at his cabin at random times or linger a while after church, flirting following the sermon. It also seemed he'd been seeing less of John and more of Frederick, who appeared just about everywhere Will went. He still didn't know if it was Frederick he'd seen on the ledge above the Crescent two weeks earlier, but ever since, he'd been walking a line of steady indecision. He felt uneasy about this place, and every instinct told him to flee. But what about the boy? He couldn't leave him here. So why did he remain? It was selfish.

Sally worked his swimming trunks down and plunged beneath the water's surface, red hair billowing as she disappeared below. He felt guilt, overshadowed by overwhelming desire.

She emerged from below, wiping the water out of her eyes.

"What's wrong?" she said.

He shook his head, breathing hard. Looking past her, he focused on the mountainous dunes beyond the shore. Old trees clung to the edges, big roots exposed like bare knuckles from a grave. During the past week, he'd had trouble sleeping, more so than usual. Every time he closed his eyes, his mind would cut from scene to scene in that movie-reel fashion, and he'd always end up seeing the four holes in the ground at the Crescent. And he'd hear John's voice, describing the drowning death of Pastor Argus Greene. When he got past the paranoia plaguing his own mind and the boy's, it still wasn't easy ascribing a reason to those massive stones buried in the ground. Best he could figure, it was just part of the Indian monument. But it didn't sit right with him.

"When you talk about leaving, it makes me sad," Sally said. "You're needed here, do you understand that? Do you know how rare that is? You're so essential to us, Will."

He pushed away from her. Her eyes were at once beautiful and feral, their blue color made all the more surreal in contrast to the red hair framing her face. "I don't feel right here," he said.

Sally kissed him. "What will I have to do to convince you?" she said. She turned, swimming toward the beach. He moved out deeper into the water. He let the minutes pass as he stared toward the blue sky. He closed his eyes, the rhythm rocking him into a trance. The steady movement of the ocean was calming. You could almost let go. But the ocean was also a source of terrible sorrow.

His mind drifted.

⌒

Will tunnels his way through the crashing surf as Aaron floats facedown in the

98

ocean. The waves batter his body, pushing Will back, but he presses on, gasping, choking, coughing on salt water as he watches his son tossed by the cresting waves. The tiny body tumbles in the Atlantic like a piece of sun-bleached driftwood.

Rose awakens. She stands up, watching.

The deserted inner tube floats away in the distance, spinning with the strong currents that pulled the boy under only minutes ago, only moments after Will lapsed into a grand mal seizure on the shore, face resting in an inch of water, sucking in mouthfuls of brine before awakening, sharp pain in his nostrils, taste of blood in his mouth, heaving and spitting up water and sand. He himself has nearly drowned. He can't believe he is alive and wishes he weren't as he realizes what is happening.

He punches his way through the white caps.

Closer and closer, he swims harder and harder, pain burning in his arms as he nears the boy's lifeless body, embracing the child, clutching the frail limbs, which dangle about. He holds onto Aaron, swimming back toward the shore. When his feet scrape the sand and rocks, Will picks the boy up and sprints, splashing through the tide.

Rose runs toward them, her wailing voice like nothing he would ever hear again.

$$\sim$$

The boy's death became regional news.

Once the medical examiner's report was complete, and the police had looked into Will's history of epilepsy, the Savannah *Daily Post* got ahold of it: "Boy Drowns During Father's Seizure." The story got picked up by the Associated Press. Reporters called Will and Rose often during that long, surreal week. Their cell phones rang constantly. One reporter in Birmingham sent a friend request to Rose's Facebook account. There were knocks at the door. The couple closed the blinds.

That evening, after opening a bottle of wine he'd discovered in a dining room cabinet, he picked up his cell phone and texted one of the reporters from the Atlanta paper. Will told him everything that happened and hit Send. Will was sad. He felt guilty. He wanted to kill himself. But it was an accident, and he had nothing to hide.

When Rose went to bed that night, Will drove to the liquor store. He bought a pint of cheap whiskey and drank most of it on the way back home. He stuck the bottle in his back pocket and stumbled inside the house. He walked to the bedroom and looked in on Rose. She stared at the ceiling, unblinking. She lay on top of the covers, still fully clothed. Her arms spread out. If she'd heard him leave and come back, she showed no sign of caring.

He left her, shuffling toward the room he'd been avoiding. When he got to the door, he reached for the bottle in his pocket. Draining the contents, he set it down at the room's threshold and walked inside.

He left the light off. Instead, he walked over to the window and raised the blinds, letting the moonlight illuminate the room. He didn't want to see anything too clearly. The bed was unmade. There were action figures scattered across the floor. A box of Legos beside the book shelf. He bent to the shelf, looking through the titles. The going-to-bed books. The counting books. The Dr. Seuss. He opened the closet and removed a cardboard box. It was full of the baby stuff they'd kept.

He sifted through the toys. There was a stuffed monkey that sang when you squeezed its belly. Baby rattles shaped like dinosaurs. There was the music box that had been attached to the crib. Will flipped a switch, and the nursery music came on. It was a lullaby rendition of a Beethoven song. Will shut it off and placed it back in the box. He folded the corners closed and shut the closet door.

He collapsed on his son's bed, the pillow smelling like Aaron's apple-scented shampoo. Glow-in-the-dark ceiling stickers blurred as he cried himself to sleep.

Just six months after her only son drowned, Rose Fordham filed for divorce. She wanted to move on, she told Will.

Will accepted the news with the same degree of withdrawal which he now reserved for all things in this world. Everything felt numb as he retreated into an existence of Xanax, antidepressants, whiskey, and seizure medication. He bought oxycodone from a friend at work. It helped sometimes. He stopped going to church, despite West Greene's weekly visits to his home. West was worried about Will and sat by his bedside encouraging him. He came by on Sunday afternoons, telling Will about the sermon. Will just stared out the window.

He tried to get clean once, but found the insomnia and lucid visions more intolerable than anything. With a clear head, he relived every second of that afternoon on the beach. To alleviate thoughts of suicide, he went back to his meds, destined to live out the rest of his existence in a stupor. He found he could still maintain his landscaping work. Just to be safe, though, he always kept at least a dozen painkillers on hand in case he decided to kill himself.

He took on even more hours. Trimming hedges, mowing grass, pruning crepe myrtles, weed-eating, planting flower bulbs, and piling mulch around plants put his mind at ease. The familiar territory and mechanical movements helped him escape a life that had gone awry. At worst, it allowed him to get away from himself for ten hours every day.

He stayed away from Grace Fellowship Church. He'd heard about Rose and her new husband. It had taken her less than a year to chart a new life with the church's new senior pastor. The congregation was sympathetic to Rose, but many took Will's absence from the church as a sign of his guilt, assigning him fault in the boy's death. With open arms, however, they welcomed Rose back.

Despite the congregation's seeming desire to forget that Will existed, West made it a point to jog their memories. When the new pastor would ask if there were any prayer requests, the old man never missed the opportunity to remind them all that they had a wounded Christian in their ranks.

—

When he was sure Sally was gone and that he was all alone on the beach, Will trudged out of the water. It was still early in the morning—two days before the pig roast—and the end of his first full month on the island. Only he seemed to notice that it had been a month, because the people of Muskogee did not use calendars, nor did they designate any day of the week as anything other than a "working day" or Sunday.

He had been spending more and more time over the past several days watching Maxwell, Esther, and the rest of the island people, observing their unique lifestyles. Not that he hadn't been watching them all along; it was just that he'd begun to feel a more pronounced distance between himself and the others. It felt as though he were sort of disappearing. It was a strange sensation.

As Will made his way up the beach, he felt a soft crunch under his right foot. Lifting it, he saw a sand dollar busted into shards, each interlocking puzzle piece its own shape. The pieces clung to his foot, glued by the briny salt water.

He brushed away the tiny marine shell and walked on, thinking about the predicament he was getting himself into with Sally. He felt a great deal of guilt about it already. She and Frederick were a couple—he was sure of that much. Here he was, the spiritual leader of the island, and he was getting involved with somebody's girlfriend. The more he thought about it, the more he realized he should probably avoid Frederick, for fear that his facial expressions might reveal the truth. Will hiked toward the sand dunes, cutting through the woods to get to his cabin—doing so meant he was less likely to cross paths with the man.

He heard something crash through the woods ahead and looked up to see a brown animal bolting away. It was one of the Muskogee hogs, namesake of the pig roast. From what he'd been told, the animals had come to the remote island along with the Spanish, who'd settled there centuries before the Campbells bought it. The creatures had flourished, much to the advantage of those on the island who had acquired a taste for them. Will watched as the animal disappeared beneath the foliage, plants waving in its wake.

"Too big," a voice said.

Will turned. Frederick stood there, holding his snarling pit bull on a leash at arm's length. The dog growled, saliva dripping from black gums. Tightening his grip on the leash, Frederick repeated himself: "The hog is too big. The older they get, the tougher they are. Taste sour."

Will had never been this close to the man, and for the first time, he noticed the faded tattoos on his arms, half-hidden by the sleeves of his shirt. On his right arm, a hula dancer. On the bicep of his left arm, an amalgamation of ink blurred by time. On his neck, Will noticed a scar. He realized too late that he'd lingered too long on the blemish.

"Yeah, one of the hogs did that," Frederick said, a slow smile spreading across his face. "He tried to kill me. I thought the motherfucker was dead." He touched the swelling of pink flesh with his hand.

"Must be scary," Will said. "They're big animals."

"It doesn't scare me," he said, pushing past Will. He yanked the leash, dragging the dog with him. The canine yelped, but followed.

Frederick took several steps, then stopped. "Be careful cutting through the woods like this. There's alligators. One of them gets you, nobody will ever find you."

CHAPTER NINE

The next day, while the island was bustling with activity and everybody was getting ready for the pig roast, Will made good on his promise to John. Taking with him a flashlight he'd borrowed from the boy and a towel inside a plastic bag, Will removed the padlock from the crawl-space door outside the plantation—it had been dummy-locked—and entered the dark depths beneath the old home.

He was doubtful that by breaking into Maxwell's bedroom he'd find any "secrets" as the boy had hoped, but he decided to do it nonetheless. Will was reluctant to admit he was doing this to prove to himself (and not to the boy) nothing was amiss.

In planning this, he hadn't factored in the awful state of the crawl space—or the smell. The narrow space reeked of sewage. It wasn't until Will was halfway through, clothing caked in mud, that his flashlight began to flicker. He tapped it against his hand, and it came on again, producing a weak beam of light. He pointed it ahead, eyeing the path. The sagging wooden floors of the old plantation home were less than a foot from the ground in some places, and he wondered if he could fit through.

The boy had described the route in great detail, and Will could see slither marks in the mud that he assumed belonged to John. But John was much tinier than Will. Holding his breath, Will pushed his way through, scraping painfully against the underside of the home. A nail sticking out of the wood caught on his back, tearing skin. He gritted his teeth and plowed ahead.

He heard something moving, a faint rustle of plastic. He sank closer to the earth, hunkering against the cool ground, eyes fixed in the direction from which he thought the sound might have come. Nobody was supposed to be home. He'd timed it that way. He'd left the group of islanders out in the field only minutes earlier, telling them he was going to study the Bible. Some were tilling the soil, while others were making decorations for the next day's event. Sally had given him a curious look but nodded. Frederick had been the only one unaccounted for all day, but Will hadn't asked where he was for fear of raising suspicion.

Maxwell and Esther had left the island earlier that morning "on business." They weren't expected to return on the courier boat until the next day. Again, he'd avoided asking questions to keep from giving away his plans. The plantation was empty for once, and it was the perfect opportunity to finally figure out if there was any truth to John's paranoia.

Will held his breath, listening for nearly a minute, before he started moving again. He assumed the strange sound had been a product of his own paranoia. He felt guilty about this. He didn't feel too good about himself. Breaking and entering wasn't something he'd ever seen himself doing.

As he started crawling again, his flashlight went out completely. Reaching up, Will grabbed ahold of one of the planks above. He lay on his back in the darkness, breathing in the shit. He heard the sound again. It was very close now. He could hear feet padding toward him, hear the ground slurping under a heavy weight.

There was someone or something down here with him. He tried to control his breathing, tried to force his eyes to adjust to the darkness. There was a thin wedge of light in the distance—the gap beneath the crawl-space door. It was too far away now to provide any illumination, but he focused on it because it was the only thing he could see.

Something tickled the back of his neck, and he swatted at it. As a landscaper, he was used to dealing with bugs. He'd seen so many snakes and spiders, he'd lost most any fear of them. But down here in the dark, it was different. And it wasn't a snake or spider making all that racket. Will breathed deeply and started crawling again, hoping he was headed in the right direction.

Propping himself up on his elbows, his back against the stone foundation, Will pushed up on the crawl-space ceiling until he found the loose boards. The dark cavity beneath lit up as he slid aside a layer of rotten particle board and caught a whiff of mothballs. The opening was small, a perfectly sized secret passageway for a young child but problematic for Will. He sucked in his breath and squeezed inside, barely fitting. He wiped the mud from his hands and face with the towel he'd brought in a plastic bag. He'd had a feeling it was going to get filthy, and he didn't want to leave muddy tracks inside the house. He placed his shoes in the plastic bag as he worked his way through the old closet.

The door creaked as he opened it and peered into the large and tidy room. There was a queen-size bed, antique nightstand, an expensive-looking dresser, and a glass-front showcase. Will walked over, peering inside the showcase. There were artifacts of all kinds inside, from Indian arrowheads to thick shards of old pottery.

A painting of Maxwell hung above the showcase. Either the portrait had been made years ago or the artist had been very kind to Maxwell, ignoring the wrinkles around his eyes and mouth. In the portrait, Maxwell held a scythe in his left hand, its blade gleaming. In the background, several men and women crouched before a field of corn. There was a signature at the bottom of the portrait: Sally Mansell.

He walked away from the showcase, glancing out the bedroom window. He could see the group of islanders working in the distance, much like in the painting. Letting the curtains fall back in place, he turned toward the dresser and rummaged through the neatly folded clothing. He searched and searched again, but found nothing inside except shirts and socks. He riffled through a stack of papers inside the nightstand. It consisted of nondescript receipts and an old business card with a law firm's name and number. The phone number had a Savannah area code. There was also a bank envelope with what looked like a house key inside. Other than that, he found very little.

He closed the drawer, noticing a spiral-bound notebook on the nightstand. He flipped through the pages, eyeing the careful precision of Maxwell Summerour's handwriting. Each page was filled with notes, and at the top of each page was a numbered date. The outside of the notebook was yellow, unremarkable. The kind you might find in a pharmacy.

He stopped at an entry dated three weeks back: "His arrival on the island has been timed perfectly. The men and women of Muskogee need religion again. It's been too long since Argus Greene passed, and Will Fordham's presence here has been a blessing. While I am not a religious man, I feel..."

It was Maxwell's journal.

He flipped to the front of the book, finding the very first entry. "The island needs a guardian. Somebody with an organized mind to keep vigil. Most importantly, Esther Campbell needs somebody to watch out for her best interests as these money-grubbing vultures circle her estate. There are those who see this island as nothing more than land waiting to be bought. Greed motivates these men. Greed, plain and simple. If they could only walk the beach here or experience the sheer serenity that surrounds..."

Will stopped. The words felt stilted, the handwriting unusual. He skimmed through several pages and began reading again: "Argus Greene, our senile reverend, tried to molest one of the islanders this afternoon. Anne Clarke entered my office this evening to announce what had happened. He'd cornered the poor girl in her cabin and begun fondling her. Frederick and I set out to find Argus to question him. After nearly three hours scouring the island, we found him sitting naked, cross-legged, in the tide pool, with scratch marks across his face. He sang hymns as the ghost crabs encircled him. It's a dangerous thing for an eighty-year-old man to go playing in the tide, and he should not be allowed to be alone anymore with these women.

"His behavior does not bode well for the people here. They see such things, and they begin to wonder if Muskogee is a safe place. Anne was inconsolable of course. She left the island. Can't say I blame her."

Will flipped through several more pages, filled mostly with dull musings about the animals and plants of the island. One four-page entry was devoted exclusively to best practices for harvesting corn. Another entry discussed the mineral deposits found in Muskogee soil. Will was about to give up before he stumbled upon something of a more personal nature: "I stole a kiss this afternoon from Esther Campbell. She is a woman of classic beauty. And she is incredible. It's fascinating to peel back the layers. She has many. On the outside, she'd have you believe that she's a charming, no-nonsense kind of woman. But when I invest time with her and put forth the effort to get her to open up, it's as if she's been waiting to find someone..."

Will skipped several lines: "I told those greedy bastards from Arch Holdings to never come back to Muskogee. They left in the same boat, the one with the corporate logo. It's surprising how little these people listen. Esther has told them time and again that she has no interest in selling the island for profit. Each time they arrive, they do so with more cajoling and even less respect for her. I'd tell them to get the hell out of here, but she wants me to be respectful to guests—even those who want to lay waste to this natural wonder.

"She's considering deeding the land to the state for green space, but I warn her to be careful of that too. Government and accountability are not often one and the same. The much-publicized green space vs. greed space debacle has left her wary, to say the least. It's for the better. But it makes you wonder who will be the steward of Muskogee. She is, after all, without any children to assume ownership. My own failure to have children as a younger man does not upset me, except that it would have been nice to see this place now through the eyes of a child. Despite our age and our likely inability to pass this island down to another generation, I am not deterred in my efforts to one day make Esther Campbell my wife."

Something banged against the side of the plantation. Will set the notebook down carefully in the exact position he'd found it in. He approached the window, peering out.

Frederick stood just below the window, only a couple feet away, hanging the padlock back on the crawl-space door.

Will was trapped inside the house.

He went back to the closet, replacing the wooden slats. Maybe he could hide somewhere. A big, old house like this had to be good for that at least. He paused, hearing the echo of footsteps inside. The wooden flooring creaked under Frederick's weight.

Holding his breath, he listened as Frederick made his way from room to room. "Somebody in here?" Frederick called out.

Will listened as the man walked from room to room and made his way up the old stairs, footsteps booming above. Will put his ear to the wall, trying to follow Frederick throughout the house. The lumber of the old home carried sound.

What would Frederick do if he found him in here, all alone in a place where he clearly wasn't supposed to be? Especially given the current state of affairs with Sally. Will knew the situation could soon come to a head. He felt sure the man would seize the opportunity to try and beat the shit out of him.

The footsteps finally stopped. Will waited, counting to one hundred and then back down to one. He emerged from the closet. The floorboards made a symphony of noises. He grimaced. Pushing Maxwell's bedroom door open just far enough to peek out, he eyed the hallway. He slipped through, pushing the door back in place, and padded through the home, trying to figure out how the hell to get out of there.

The place was scary. Any natural light that could have illuminated the inside of the building had been blocked out by large burgundy-colored curtains for which there seemed to be no good reason. As somebody who had seen visions and apparitions often throughout his life, Will waited for the inevitable. In a place like this, you were bound to see something awful. The old furniture was so rotten, so engulfed in mold and cobwebs, that he wondered how anyone could stand to live here among it all. Why did Maxwell keep his bedroom and office so clean but leave all of this to rot?

There was also the smell. With notes of whatever had gone wrong with the crawl-space plumbing, there was a scent of dead animal, of plant decay and old clothes. It all swirled together in a way that was offensive not only to the senses but to the mind as well. It was an odor that chilled him to the core. It was what ghosts smelled like. Not innocent spirits trapped in some nebulous state of otherness, but devils with wicked intent.

Will bumped around in the near darkness. He was utterly lost, but after several minutes he was able to find the front door. Approaching the large entrance and putting his hand on the knob, he heard the familiar voice: "Come on out."

Will swallowed hard and stepped out of the door.

"I won't even ask what you're doing in there," Frederick said, reclining in a rocking chair. He held a massive knife in one hand, whittling the tip of a long piece of fresh wood. Will could smell the green sapling's blood. On Frederick's belt, there was a gun holster with a big pistol in it.

"I was just trying to find—"

"We got business to attend to," Frederick said. He banged the newly sharpened wooden spear against the deck and stood up.

Will nodded. His instincts urged him to bolt for the woods. He could make it if he ran fast. Or could he? He eyed Frederick, who shook his head as if reading Will's every thought. "You got any clue what I'm talking about, Reverend?"

"I just need to get back to my cabin."

He approached Will, placing a rough hand on his shoulder. "Well, that ain't happening. You're part of all this now."

"I haven't done anything to you."

Frederick tilted his head. A flicker of contempt crossed the man's face, and Will felt his hands shake. It was that old familiar rush of adrenaline preceding a situation like this. Will knew that with someone as physically imposing as Frederick, he'd have to be the one to throw the first punch, and that punch would have to be dirty. Will's father had taught him to fight when he was a boy. He'd said that when two men fought, it was the one who let all the demons out, the one who fought the dirtiest, who would always win. These weren't Christian thoughts, though. Jesus taught to turn the other cheek. Will decided it would be better for him to just get out of there before it came to a fight, and he watched for the right opportunity.

He followed Frederick down the steps. Out of the corner of his eye, Will could see the large knife in Frederick's hand. "You're lucky I seen you when I did," said Frederick. "Or rather, you're lucky Stark seen you."

"Stark?"

They rounded the corner of the plantation. The pit bull was tethered to a tree. The animal stared at the crawl-space door, growling. "Yeah, Stark," said Frederick. The dog looked up at the mention of his name and took several steps back. "He started barking, and I came over and seen it."

Frederick took off the padlock and snapped open the crawl-space door, shining a flashlight into the dark. He waved the beam from corner to corner until a smile appeared on his face. It was the first time Will had seen the man look so happy. Frederick waved a hand, motioning for him to come over. When Will peered inside he saw a massive alligator in the corner of the crawl space, its body wedged against the home's foundation. The reptile hid in the mud, regarding Will with fear in its eyes.

CHAPTER TEN

They walked together through the woods, Will lagging behind. Watching Frederick and Stark lead the way, he waited for the right moment to run. They'd ventured off the gravel trail, twigs snapping under their shoes as they made their way toward the island's center. The deep woods were dangerous, he'd been told. Alligators usually didn't venture so far from the swamp, but the Muskogee hogs were big, and the bobcats were rumored to not fear people. The further they walked, the more Will's sense of direction failed him. It seemed they were hiking in circles.

"Back at the house, you said you ain't done nothing to me," Frederick said, crunching through the foliage. "What did you mean by that?"

Will glanced around him, eyeing gaps in the thickening forest. Frederick stopped, yanking the dog's leash. Stark yelped, then sat down, looking up at his master with pale blue eyes. The pit bull had a slate-gray coat of fur with a white stripe running down his face.

"Is this about Sally jerking you off in the ocean? That what you're talking about?"

Will felt the anger flare, hearing the crude way Frederick talked about her. He balled up his fists. Frederick had been spying on them.

He knew it. The adrenaline raced as he looked Frederick in the eyes.

A smile spread across the man's face. "Man of God, my ass."

Frederick was big. No, he was huge. But Will was strong. He would never win a fight against him, but it would be worth it to punch him. Bust his face wide open, take his gun away. His anger had emboldened him. As if reading Will's mind, Frederick unsheathed his knife, gripping it with a large fist. He pushed the handle of the spear toward Will. "Use this," Frederick said.

"What? What for? What are we doing out here?"

Frederick ignored the question, and with much confusion, Will took the spear. The wind picked up, a breeze blowing cold against his face. He could feel natural forces shifting. The clouds were coming together, a cold front moving in from somewhere. His sense of hearing felt muffled. Sound came in waves. It was the dulling of his everyday perceptions that made way for that sixth and mysterious sense. His head throbbed and his mouth turned dry as he gripped the weapon.

"There's a storm coming," Will said.

"Well, hell. We better get a move on."

Will followed Frederick. The tip of the spear dragged in the dirt behind him. The forest grew stranger. The trees formed an archway, a canopy of dark branches. The palmetto plants grew big and thick, with jagged green fronds reaching six feet tall. Will became aware of a crunching sound beneath his feet and noticed tiny round stones on the ground. They were the kind of pebbles you found in a mountain stream. Black and gray. Smooth.

They walked on for nearly a mile. The scent of turned earth wafted in the breeze, a rich barnyard stench like grass and manure.

"This way," Frederick said, cutting away from the trail now. They walked down a smaller path. The ground was softer. Will pushed limbs aside as he followed close behind. They came to a break in the foliage. Will glanced around at the ruins of a small building's foundation. A tall pile of bricks rose up from the ground beside them, a crumbled chimney. Deformed saplings grew from it. Vines encircled the chimney like interlocking fingers pulling it toward the earth.

"Slave quarters," Frederick said, answering an unasked question. He walked past the chimney, pointing at a sunken mud pit beside it. "They roam, they sleep, and they play. This is where they play."

It was then that Will understood the purpose of their journey. It was the day before the pig roast, and they needed fresh meat. Frederick needed somebody strong to help hunt and drag the kill back to their camp.

He followed Frederick past the chimney, toward the edge of the forest. The air opened up around them as they stepped into the sunlight. Will was startled by what he saw. For a moment, he thought he was dreaming. About twenty yards in front of them were the remnants of the largest mansion he had ever seen. Twin chimneys on either side of the building rose up, jutting their way into the sky.

"What is this?" Will asked, stumbling along behind Frederick. They walked past an empty fountain made of gray stone. Tall weeds sprang up from cracks inside it.

"Summer home of the Rockefellers," Frederick said. "Believe it or not."

They stepped through a grand entrance with pillars on either side. Dark stains of corrosion encircled the tall stone entryway. Lush trees of all variety shaded their walk. Will also noticed the enormous roses. The buds were otherworldly, the size of softballs, with thorns as thick as his pinky finger.

"The Rockefellers were in New York when the storm came," Frederick said. "They heard what happened and never came back. That's what I been told anyway. Their plants kept growing, though. Ever seen a rosebush like that?"

Will shook his head. He gazed with awe at a series of trellis systems almost as expansive as a football field. The curling fingers of muscadine vines covered what seemed like every inch of the field. The fat, purple grapes were ripe. Will walked to the edge of the field and plucked several. He popped them in his mouth, tasting the sweet explosion of juice on his tongue. "So the whole island really flooded?"

"That's right." Frederick said, using the bottom of his T-shirt to gather muscadines. "Late 1800s, something like that. That's what they say, anyway."

Will examined the ruins. All that remained was a skeleton of stonework. It had once spanned what he could only guess was ten thousand square feet of living space.

"Nothing here but them hogs now," Frederick offered.

They approached an east-facing room of the mansion, where a large chimney stood tall. The brick ventilation ducts were the only structures seemingly untouched by time. Frederick thrust his hand in front of Will's chest as they neared the room's threshold. He yanked on Stark's leash, and the dog sat down and growled. There was a snorting and a staccato belching coming from inside. Small puffs of dust rose from a corner hidden from view.

"Sounds like two little ones," Frederick breathed. And then, peering around the corner, he got a better look. "We're gonna do this the fun way. You go right. I'll go left."

He tied Stark's leash to a small tree that had grown up inside the ruins. He held up three fingers. Two fingers. One. "Go," he whispered.

Frederick and Will popped out from behind the corner, where

two small hogs were caught by surprise. They bucked, squealing madly, as they trampled the dust. Frederick lunged on top of the first one and cut its throat. Will missed his chance to spear the other small hog, which bolted past him. It cleared a large pile of stones, disappearing.

"Damn it," Frederick bellowed, blood spritzing his face. Frederick held onto the small hog, its muscles twitching. He wiped the knife blade in the dirt and stood up. "Well, hell," Frederick said. "Two little ones might have done it, but now we gotta go and find some more. Nice hunting there, buddy."

Frederick disappeared into the woods, leaving Will alone with the dead-eyed baby Muskogee hog. It had a wrinkled snout and calico coloring. Already, flies swarmed its mouth and eyeballs. He saw Frederick coming back through the woods, carrying two freshly cut saplings and several handfuls of wild vine. Will helped Frederick tie the hog and secure it to the wooden branches, making a sort of stretcher with which to drag it back to the colony.

"Now, let's just go ahead and clear the air," Frederick said. "You think you done wrong by me with this whole Sally thing. Truth is, Sally don't belong to me. I was just giving you a hard time, that's all."

Will didn't know what to say. He'd been prepared for anything except reconciliatory words from Frederick. He was skeptical. Why make such a big deal about it earlier if it wasn't an issue?

Frederick laughed. "Look at you. All paranoid. I ain't such a bad guy, you know."

Will finished tying the animal's hooves to the limbs, and looked beyond the man, peering into the woods. He was at a loss for words.

Without warning, Frederick unholstered his gun and leveled the barrel just above Will's eyes. The bore was dark and cavernous. It was the end. He'd been tricked, and it was a hell of a trick, too. Drag him out here in the middle of nowhere, take him out with a single bullet. Make them think it was a hunting accident. Let the animals tear his body apart. He shut his eyes, ready for whatever came next. Between a man and a gun, there was no room for fighting.

The gunshot nearly deafened him. A sound like a strangled roar followed, and there was an intense ringing in his ears. He opened his eyes to see Frederick pushing past him toward the twitching body of a hundred-pound mother Muskogee hog. Blood oozed from the fresh hole in its head.

CHAPTER ELEVEN

It was at some point during their walk back through the woods, while helping Frederick drag the bloodied baby hog and its mother back to the colony, that Will decided it was time to leave. He wasn't doing anybody any good here—certainly not himself. Though he'd been pondering the notion of leaving for a couple weeks now, the decision now came suddenly, and he wanted to act before changing his mind yet again.

The next morning, back at his cabin, he moved quickly. He tossed his clothing and other belongings into his duffle bags and cleaned up what little mess he'd made, sweeping sand from the floors with a broom he'd found in the closet. He knew Maxwell and Esther would be arriving at the pier that afternoon; he could ride back to Savannah on the returning boat.

Several hours later, he stood at the edge of the waters watching the vessel arrive, thinking how strange it was that everything he owned could fit inside three duffle bags. Well, one was really more of a satchel, a big blue bag with his initials embroidered on it. It had been a wedding gift from one of Will's old friends who'd stopped coming around after the divorce was finalized. People were like that, weren't they? To be shunned by his old church friends had made him feel like he had some disease. It also intensified the guilt he felt following the tragedy, as if it were indeed all his fault, and the ostracism had been part of God's punishment.

As the boat drew nearer, rocking up and down against fierce waves, he could see the silhouettes of Maxwell, Esther, and the boat's captain. In his haste to leave, Will had not considered what he might give Maxwell as a reason for his sudden departure. Telling the man that he doubted the existence—or at the very least, the intentions—of God might be a good start. Or he could say that he felt just as useless here as he had back in Savannah. But the truth was that he owed Maxwell no explanation. He owed nothing to anyone—except he still felt an obligation to John. He wanted to help the boy somehow, even if the paranoid tales of murder were manufactured. If nothing else, the fabrications were a cry for help. John didn't seem to want to be here, nor did it seem he belonged.

In any case, it was something he could figure out when he got back to Savannah. Maybe he could find some way to get custody of John. It wasn't likely he'd get much of a fight from Sally. Shouldn't John be in a public school system? Shouldn't he be in a place where there were other children to play with? The whole thing seemed wrong, and he felt responsible for whatever happened to the boy. But for the time being, he just needed to get as far away from Muskogee as possible. He had to get his head clear again.

Winds picked up as the boat arrived. Maxwell waved, a look of surprise on his face. But then his self-assured smile sank, deflated by the sight of the bags.

Will looked past him, stepping onto the boat as the couple stepped off. He nodded to Amos McGuire. "I need a ride back to

Savannah," Will said.

"Sure, buddy," said Amos.

Will dropped his luggage with a thud and sank into a chair. The seat was wet from the ocean mist. "Well, this is such a surprise," Maxwell managed, setting down his briefcase. "Are you going for a day trip? Need to get some supplies? Esther and I, we would be glad to get whatever you need."

"It's not working out," Will said. "This was a mistake. I'm sorry for wasting everybody's time."

Maxwell looked flummoxed. This man who so readily spoke in any given situation was at last speechless.

Will looked at the captain. "Can we go?"

The captain nodded, cranking the engine. The vessel vibrated beneath Will's sneakers. The kinetic energy made him feel strange. He was escaping again, this time in a way that was bullshit. He was fooling himself if he thought this would change a thing. Liberation, though, seemed to lie in the act of transition. The promise of motion made him feel free again, no matter how fleetingly. The future be damned. He didn't know what lay ahead, but the way things were going, it probably wouldn't be good. There would be drinking. There would be medication. So much medication. It was an illusion to live life like that, but it was comfortable, and it had the power to make him forget. If he left the island now, he was headed back into the old, familiar rut. Still, though, it had to be better than this place.

Out of the corner of his eye, Will saw Maxwell hand Amos some money. He said something out of Will's earshot. The engine shuddered to a stop. Amos gave Will an apologetic look and stepped off the boat, lighting a cigarette.

"Listen," Maxwell said to Will. "If things aren't working out, that's fine. If you need to leave us, then I won't hold that against you. We'll miss you. You've been a fantastic person to have around. Your spiritual leadership has meant the world to these people. I know Sally will certainly miss you. You're all she talks about."

Will listened, looking out over the water.

"And that boy," Maxwell continued. "He idolizes you, Sally tells me."

"We need you, sweetheart," Esther said to Will. "Maxwell and I are getting married."

"Congratulations," Will said. "But you don't need me for that."

Maxwell sighed. "Actually, we do. The wife-to-be here won't get married without a Christian ceremony. We just got back from probate court. We've got the paperwork ready to go, just need the signature of an officiating pastor. Now, I know you're ordained. West told me you were."

"Yeah, I'm ordained," Will said. "But there's plenty of pastors on the mainland. You can find somebody else."

Esther smiled. "I want somebody I can trust, Will. Not just any Christian pastor. I want this to be right in the eyes of the Lord. I want it to be right for my deceased husband, who's looking down from heaven. When I met you, I knew it was going to be you. I knew it was God's plan."

Will looked at Maxwell, who shrugged his shoulders. "She's very particular about this," he said. "All you've got to do is stay one more day. We can do the ceremony this evening, you can sign the papers, and go back home tomorrow. Amos here, he's got to come back anyway. I'm going back to probate court to deliver the papers after you sign them. That will make it official." Maxwell held up his briefcase, gesturing toward the captain. "What time can you come back tomorrow, Mr. Amos?"

"Noon," Amos said. "Unless you need me sooner."

Esther leaned toward Will. "Please. I can't tell you how important this is. Do me this one favor, and then you can go back home."

⸻

Clutching his Bible, Will stared from the edge of the woods near his cabin. He'd stopped to watch Frederick on the way back from the wedding ceremony. Frederick tied the dead mother hog to palm branches beside the commons area. He hung the animal upside down. Will watched the preparations, observing the near mechanical precision with which Frederick butchered the creature.

It had been the first and only time Will officiated a wedding, and it was awkward. He'd had to wing it for much of the ceremony, trying to remember what he was supposed to say. There was a whole class he'd taken at seminary school that prepared pastors for such events, but it all seemed so long ago. Memory failed him.

Maxwell and Esther hadn't seemed to mind. When Will had put his signature on the marriage license, Esther kissed him on the cheek. Maxwell looked even happier. He beamed at Will, thrusting a firm handshake upon him. "We'll show you a great time tonight, friend," he said. "You'll be glad you stayed. I'll make sure it's worth your while." The pig roast included a night of drinking and dancing, he'd been told, and he wouldn't mind having a drink or two tonight. Just a little something to calm his nerves.

"Give me a hand over here," Frederick called out suddenly. "Cut those ropes. Help me drag it to the table."

Frederick stood beneath the dead animal, bracing it for impact as Will slashed the ropes. They lifted the hog and set it on the picnic table. Frederick used a sharp knife to strip hair from the animal's body. He moved the blade with stealth, finely shearing the skin's surface.

They dragged the carcass back to the tree and hung it again. Frederick removed another knife, this one much larger, and made two fast slashes at the belly. The animal's guts spilled from its torso. "Thanks," Frederick called out. "Hey, you got company."

Will turned and saw Sally standing at the entrance to his cabin in a dirty smock, watching them. She had an easel tucked under her arm and a paint-stained canvas bag slung over her shoulder. Will glanced back at Frederick, but the man didn't seem concerned. He plunged his hands repeatedly into the pig's stomach, removing entrails. He slung pink, yellow, and blue cords of tissue into the dirt.

Will followed Sally into the cabin.

—

"Looks like y'all had a successful hunt," Sally said, squeezing colorful globs of paint onto a wooden palette. She stood before the easel and canvas, lost in the ritual of preparation. A cool wind blew from the open window behind her as she worked the tubes with her fingers.

"Yeah," Will said. "A wedding and a butchering all on the same day."

Sally looked up, the faintest smile disappearing from her lips. "Oh. Yes, well, Frederick takes his work very seriously."

"I'm not denying that. He's good. For a second, I thought he was going to butcher me."

"Why would you think that?"

"You still haven't told me where y'all stand."

"I told you. We don't put—"

"Yeah, yeah. You don't put labels on anything."

"Sit down," she said. "Right there, on the bed. I can't paint you if you keep moving around. Try and relax."

Her eyes narrowed as she got to work on the portrait, making broad strokes. Will tried to relax, but he was angry. He had never been the type of person to take relationships lightly. Intimacy was a sacred thing. Letting people in wasn't easy for Will. In fact, it got harder every time. He'd been hurt before by women like Sally, and he wasn't going to fall into the trap. If what she wanted from him was purely physical, he'd offer her nothing less.

But the truth was, he was hurting. Sally was the first woman who'd offered him anything more than sympathy since Rose had left him. And he was kidding himself if he thought that didn't get to him. He didn't understand Sally. He didn't really trust her, if he was being honest. But he liked her. He couldn't help it. She was interesting. She was an enigma. She was a beautiful woman. She was charming. What kind of man would he be if that stuff didn't get to him, if those things didn't cut him to the core?

"I'm leaving tomorrow," Will said.

Carefully, she set the palette down on a table beside her. Wiping her hands, Sally removed the paint-stained smock. "Is it something I said?"

He looked out the open window as she approached him. She straightened his shirt, smoothed the cowlick on the back of his hair. She leaned down to his eye level, locking him with those eyes. "Listen, you've got to relax. I'll never finish this if you're just sitting there pouting."

She placed a hand on his leg.

"I don't want this," he said.

She undid his belt buckle, pushing him down on the mattress. "Well, I do."

She took her clothes off. Her body was perfect. Even more perfect than he'd imagined. He wanted her so badly. As she laid down on the bed beside him, she picked up the old Bible from his nightstand, giggling as she flipped through the pages.

She cleared her throat, raising light-colored eyebrows: "Be ye not unequally yoked together with unbelievers. For what fellowship hath righteousness with unrighteousness? And what communion hath light with darkness?"

Her eyes flickered toward Will's, large and blue. Easing onto her side, she tossed the Bible. It hit the floor with a thud, pages splayed.

She climbed on top of him, pinning his shoulders. They fucked. His mind seemed to turn off as he fell into the rhythmic motion. She sank her fingernails into the back of his neck. Sally moaned, her breath coming in hurried gasps. Will was sure everyone on the island could hear them. They moved together at a frantic pace for what felt like hours.

In the sound of his own ragged voice, Will thought he heard the younger version of himself. The young man losing his virginity to Rose seven years ago, a month before their wedding. Inside the home of her parents, who'd left the couple alone to run errands. They were making out in her bedroom, when something had come over him. He became possessed by this desire. His rational mind was eclipsed by the primitive act. She'd not been a virgin, and she didn't want to marry a virgin, she said. Marrying a pastor was bad enough.

Now, out of breath, Will climbed off the bed.

Sally got out of bed and put her clothes back on. "Are you going to the pig roast tonight?" she said, buttoning her shorts.

He picked the Bible up from the floor, looking at his name imprinted in gold letters on the cover. If he thought back far enough, he could remember the Christmas morning when he'd received the brand-new Bible. He'd hated it at first. Other kids got video games and toys. But over the years, he'd developed a fondness for it. The familiar streaks of yellow highlighter and the pencil scratches where he'd underlined verses—they were like the idiosyncrasies of an old friend.

But it meant nothing to him now. That was someone else's life. He set the book on the nightstand, his hand shaking.

CHAPTER TWELVE

The man they called the Teacher was handing out joints. He came by the picnic table where Will sat, offering one as a party favor for the pig roast. He looked surprised when Will gratefully accepted it.

"You know how to do this, pastor?" he asked, flicking a Bic lighter.

Will leaned forward, inhaling deeply. He held the smoke in his lungs as long as he could, then coughed harshly, doubling over with each spasm. In truth, it had been a while since he smoked pot. He and his roommate in seminary school had taken an open-minded stance on recreational drugs like marijuana. They'd smoked on at least a dozen Friday nights, stoned out of their minds watching late-night television. He and the fellow twenty-year-old Bible-school student saw it as a natural thing put on the earth by God to be enjoyed in moderation, much like beer, wine, or coffee.

This wasn't moderation, Will thought, as he smoked the joint down to a tiny glowing ember. He stubbed it out on his dinner plate, higher than he'd ever been.

He sat alone beside an empty picnic table in the commons area. Seated in a metal folding chair before a great spread of food, he stared at the decapitated head of the Muskogee hog, its crisp brown skin glistening in the moonlight. Many of the others had already left the gathering, having feasted before he arrived. He'd spent some time alone in his cabin after Sally left, debating whether or not to go.

A few drunk islanders danced around a bonfire in the center of the commons area. The flames rose high, smoke billowing toward the heavens. The blaze looked like a great, diabolic blossom in the darkness.

Many of those who'd been there when Will arrived had left, but he had no idea where they'd gone. Standing up, Will grabbed a gallon jug of purple liquid from off the table. He unscrewed the cap and drank straight from the container, gulping down the mixture of water, Kool-Aid powder, and homebrewed corn liquor. The ground seemed to sink beneath his feet. He wiggled his toes, feeling the sand.

The Muskogee hog's head seemed to leer at him, half-smiling as if interrupted in the middle of telling a good joke. The animal's face was missing large chunks of flesh where islanders had torn off pieces. Its eyes were sad, sunken caverns. Just above the empty sockets was a large bullet hole.

"Get enough to eat?" Maxwell said, approaching.

Will turned and looked up as Maxwell clapped him on the shoulder. He felt like he was seeing everything with new eyes. His senses felt dull, but it seemed the world was lighting up all around him in strange ways. Maxwell's eyes glowed like twin fires in the dark as he breathed out smoke, cackling.

Will tipped the jug again, belching.

"Well, it certainly seems like you're having fun," said Maxwell. "I'm glad. Your service to our cause has been invaluable. A night of fun is the least we can do for you."

"It doesn't matter."

"Sorry?"

Will laughed. He turned the gallon jug up again and gulped the contents down like water. His thirst was unquenchable. He slammed the container down on the edge of the table. It fell off, spilling into the dirt. "Whoops."

Maxwell took a flask from his pocket. "Plenty where that came from." He tipped it up.

"You just have to understand something about me first," said Will. "I have powers, okay?"

The words hung in silence.

"Is that right?" said Maxwell.

"I am a prophet."

"You are a prophet," Maxwell said, the inflection somewhere between a statement and a question.

"But not just any prophet," Will said. He climbed up on the picnic table. "I can see the weather!" Will laughed, arms outstretched to the sky.

"Here's to the prophet!" Maxwell laughed, raising his flask in a toast.

"Cold fronts and warm fronts. Meteorology might have been better for me. A better fit. There's money in that." Will climbed down from the table.

"And what do your mighty, prophetic powers tell you tonight?" Maxwell asked.

"Storms. Bad, bad storms are coming your way, Maxwell Summerour."

"How unfortunate," Maxwell said. "Nothing worse than bad weather to ruin a festival."

Will listened as Maxwell went on to describe the pig roast ceremony in further detail. But he got distracted. He started thinking about John. The guilt about leaving without him crept into his thoughts, spoiling the mindless bliss. Where was John tonight? Had they locked him up somewhere? Was he going to try and escape and come find Will again? He didn't think he could handle that. More talk about dead people. *Murderers.*

"One thing I never got around to asking you," Will said, interrupting Maxwell. "How come John can't go down to the Crescent? He told me about your little moonlight meetings. What's the big secret? Why is it off-limits or whatever?"

Maxwell smiled vaguely. "Would you like to see why?"

⌒

"You have to understand that it was out of respect for your religious position that we never took you on this part of the tour," Maxwell said as the two made their way through the woods. "I didn't want to offend our new pastor."

As they walked, Will's mind struggled between moments of lucidity and inebriation. He was certain there was a great storm coming. It felt unlike anything he'd ever sensed. The air was charged with a fierce energy. Looking up between the branches, he saw shadows in the trees, flitting like demonic bats. He stumbled along, intermittently looking up to see if they were still there. After a few minutes, the visions changed. They became less menacing, like watching a juvenile puppet show. The kind they used to do in children's church at Grace Fellowship.

"Not exactly Christian things going on here," Maxwell continued. "But you asked, Will, so here we are."

He followed Maxwell until they came to a clearing. The two men walked along the beach. The stones of the Crescent loomed in the darkness ahead of them like the burly shoulders of giants, silhouettes framed against the purple night sky.

Will heard something as they approached. It sounded like someone crying. As they got closer, he realized there were two people lying in the center of the Crescent having sex. One of them was Frederick, and the other was a twentysomething girl he'd seen around but had never spoken to.

Frederick glanced up, his eyes squinting. He looked Will and Maxwell over and laughed. The girl rose up from the ground, turning her head. "Don't let us intrude," Maxwell said. "Just giving our young pastor the full tour."

Frederick picked up a red Solo cup beside him, drained the contents, and resumed. The girl groaned.

"You see why we can't let the boy down here. We try and reserve the more adult activities for the Crescent," Maxwell said. He gestured toward two other naked bodies several yards away. Waves crashed at their feet.

Maxwell nodded to a woman approaching them. "Will, I want you to meet Brandi."

"We've met," she said, cutting Maxwell off. She was naked, her athletic figure like a specter in the luminous night. She flaunted her body without shame. What shocked Will wasn't her nudity; it was the change in her hairstyle since the last time they'd spoken. She ran a hand across a newly shaved scalp. "How do you like it?" she asked.

They walked together toward the ocean. He sloshed along beside her, stepping through the waves in a stoned and drunken trance, still wearing his khaki pants and button-up shirt. When they were chest deep in the surf, she kissed him. The waters pushed and pulled at their bodies. Stringy, fibrous plankton and algae swirled around them, entangling his arms and legs. It felt like an ocean of human hair dancing across his skin.

"Are you cold?" She wrapped her arms around him and kissed him again. Her mouth tasted like bubble gum and cigarettes. He moved his hands across her scalp. Feeling the coarse sandpaper texture, he drew back. She giggled and took hold of him. The marijuana and liquor had a dehumanizing effect on the act. She thrust against him, pushing herself faster and faster. She leapt up into his arms, her legs straddling his body. Salt water splashed around them. He reciprocated, feeling his body building toward the moment. Will collapsed against her, his seed dispersing into the Atlantic Ocean.

She left, her tan back glistening in the moonlight as she swam through the surf. The guilt crept up on him. It had all happened so quickly, and it was as if he hadn't thought about any of it at all. Feelings of self-hatred flooded his mind. He didn't even know this woman. He paddled out deeper into the ocean, having never felt so lost in his life.

———

Upon returning to the cabin, Will repacked his clothes in the duffle bags. Trying to shake off the inebriation, he stumbled around the living space. He wished he had some coffee. Glancing at his mattress, he suddenly remembered the box beneath his bed full of photos, Howard Mansell's news clippings, and John's binoculars. He'd completely forgotten about that when packing his stuff earlier. With care, he tucked the Tupperware container into one of the duffle bags. He would take it back to John's hiding place the next morning, he decided, to keep the others from finding it and to keep John out of trouble.

Before lying down to go to sleep, he noticed Sally's half-finished portrait propped against the wall. Smears of yellow and brown paint framed Will's hair line: long tangles of blond hair tucked behind his ears. Broad strokes of bronze across the high cheekbones, the square, muscular jaw. Sally had stopped just before finishing his eyes. They were hollow pools of black. He looked dead. The longer he stared at the painting, the more it shifted. The more he focused on it, the less it looked like him, and the more it looked like the face of a stranger.

Will collapsed into bed, head spinning. He clutched at the sheets. The linens smelled of sour body odor. He pushed them aside, opening his eyes to stare out the open door frame. The palm trees swayed in the breeze.

The wind itself seemed to utter secrets to him, warnings about what was to come. Will laughed, realizing his entire life was built around unfounded premonitions. His decision to become a spiritual leader was based on the notion that he had some communion with the spiritual realm. His ability to sense those things which others could not fathom made a believer of him, and it had inspired many around him. Yet during the one time in his thirty years on this planet when he should have seen danger coming, these abilities failed him.

⌒

He awoke suddenly, feeling someone in the room with him. It was dark, but moonlight shone through the windows, spreading strange patterns across the walls. He looked at the furniture around him, examining the silhouettes. The familiar shapes of the chest of drawers, the nightstand, and an old food pantry seemed to sway in the night. He was still high, and he felt nauseated by the movement.

At the foot of his bed, he saw the slumped shoulders and tiny body of his son. He blinked, trying to ward off the hallucination. Will was afraid of what the boy might say, and he felt sick, but still he wanted to reach out and touch Aaron. He cried, burying his face in the sheets. "I'm sorry," he said. The sobs nearly choked him.

The sickness overtook him, and Will got out of bed, crawling toward the front door. Making his way outside on his hands and knees, he vomited beside the porch, his chest flashing with pain.

Collapsing, he fell asleep outside.

He had good dreams, memories of his visit to the doctor's office with Rose, seeing his baby on the sonogram. Hearing the tiny, rapid echo of his heartbeat. A rush of pride had swelled inside him as the nurse said, "It's a boy." He relived the infant months of Aaron's childhood. The child couldn't yet sleep through the night without milk. Those sleepy but sacred moments as he rocked Aaron back to sleep, lullabies humming from the music box beside the cradle.

Will awoke clutching a blanket, his neck throbbing and his body aching as he cringed at the sounds of wildlife. Birds shrieked. The forest shook with hidden creatures. It seemed to be midmorning. The wind was blowing. His face was sticky with humidity. His mouth was so dry it felt painful to swallow.

The sky was yellow.

The events of the previous evening came back to him, but only in fragments. All of it felt disjointed and distant, like a story he'd been told but could barely remember. He entered the cabin. Someone was in his bed, covers heaped over them. He crept over, pulling the sheets away.

John blinked his eyes, waking up. He sat up in Will's bed, a puzzled look spreading across his face. He glanced suspiciously through the window at the strange-colored skies. "What were you doing last night? You were acting weird."

"Last night..."

"I came in here and tried to wake you up."

"You came in here while I was asleep?"

"You kept calling me Aaron. Hey, why are your bags all packed?"

Will shook his head. "Listen, I've got to go away for a while. I'm coming back, okay? I just don't know when."

"Take me with you," John pleaded. "They're going to kill me, just like the others."

Will shook his head, feeling agitated. His head was killing him. "Why do you keep telling me this stuff?"

"Because you can help me. You've got powers. I saw it in the church. Everybody was scared, even Maxwell."

"It was just a seizure. It's a medical condition. That's one of the reasons I've got to go back home."

"God sent you here to help me."

Will shook his head. "I can't help you. Not right now."

Tears welled up in John's eyes.

"You're safe here, okay? Nobody wants to hurt you. I have to leave. I'm sorry."

Will picked up his duffle bags and left.

⌒

Will hated himself, but he wouldn't give the kid false hope. He had to get back to Savannah, at least for the time being. When he arrived there, he could regroup and try to figure out how he might help the boy. He'd do it legally too, find John a foster home. West had connections. At the very least, maybe West could offer him advice about how to get John out of the situation. It was, after all, a bad situation for a kid.

He made his way toward the pier. He wasn't sure what time it was but figured he had some time before the courier boat arrived at noon. His head throbbed with pain. This was a hangover like no other, but there was something else to it too. He tried to concentrate, but his mind wasn't working right. He'd really gotten fucked up beyond repair last night.

Stopping, he repositioned the duffle-bag straps on his shoulders. Suddenly, he remembered something: The Tupperware container with all John's belongings was inside one of his bags. If only he'd remembered a moment ago, he could have given it to him. He gave a tired sigh, turning to see how far he was from the boy's secret hiding place. He knew he wouldn't have time to try and track John down, but if he was quick about it, he could still make it to the hiding place and back before the boat arrived. He unzipped the bag, removing the Tupperware box. Setting the duffle bags down on the trail, he tucked the container beneath his arm and jogged. He could move quicker without the luggage, and he would come back for it on his way back to the pier.

Thunder cracked loudly and lightning popped as he arrived at the mouth of the hidden trail. He slowed his pace as he eyed the ground. The trail wasn't easy to follow without the boy guiding him. He looked for landmarks to help him navigate. He stomped through the foliage, going as fast as he could. At one point, Will thought he heard someone behind him. Looking back, he saw nobody and realized his mind was probably playing tricks. Nothing new there.

When he got to the end of the trail, where the jagged rock cliff overlooked the Atlantic, he looked down at the beach. The waves were massive. Whitecaps crested more than a dozen feet high. The bad weather was coming, that was for sure. It was closing in fast. He hoped it wouldn't keep the courier boat from coming though. He considered going back and warning John about the weather. He just couldn't leave him here with whatever horrifying storm was coming.

There was motion below. Will looked down and spotted someone on the beach. Three people, actually. Two of them stood in the surf, while another sat in the sand near the Crescent. Unsnapping the Tupperware container, he found John's binoculars and used them for a better view. Esther Campbell sat on the beach below, the tide crashing around her. She lounged near the shallow tide pool toward the open end of the Crescent. The tide was retreating now, waters barely above her legs as the salt water rushed beneath her. He noticed that her posture looked unnatural.

Will got a sickening feeling.

He scanned the surf with his binoculars. He stopped on the blurry shapes of two people in the water. Focusing, he saw it was Sally and Maxwell. They stood together in the rushing waters, bodies half submerged. They were kissing.

Will's heart beat swiftly as the scene made its mark. He felt nauseous. He glanced back toward Esther. The woman was lying down on her back now, facing the sky. It was then that he saw a strange movement around her head. He focused the binoculars, examining the purple color of her skin, the pouting of her lips, and what he suddenly realized was a ghost crab burrowing out of her eye socket, sheathed in dark blood.

The crab dove as a wave crashed against Esther's body and sucked the crustacean back into the Atlantic. The force of the water moved the old woman back into an upright position. The tide pulled on her like a puppet. She was bound to the rocks beneath the sand.

Will felt dizzy, putting hands on his knees. Trying to steady himself, he breathed deeply. He had to get to the boy, he thought, if they hadn't already gotten to him first. Will could feel the darkness closing in all around him. His palms sweated, head aching as he dropped the binoculars in the dirt. The symptoms of a seizure were upon him, weakening his senses. He did not hear Frederick approaching from behind.

CHAPTER THIRTEEN

Panic seized Will when he awoke. He could hear birds squalling, their frantic cries like sirens. The ocean surf crashed at his feet, water soaking his clothes and filling his shoes. He blinked up at the insane clouds that spread out above him like a great, festering wound in the sky. He turned to his right and left, seeing the rippling waters of the tide pool that surrounded him. The tide was coming in. Small, white crabs raced back and forth. He screamed, suddenly feeling the cold flesh beneath him.

He was sprawled out at the base of the Crescent, bound to the corpse of Esther Campbell.

Two men spoke loudly, shouting at one another over the clamorous surf. Will yanked at the vines. The sky darkened as the low clouds moved in, tumbling breakers matching the billowing black and blue formations above. Thunder exploded. Lightning bolts danced a spasm across the horizon.

Maxwell stepped into his line of sight, frowning. "You were certainly right about that storm," he said.

Will pushed against Esther, trying to break free, using his torso for leverage. He sank back against her. He turned angry eyes toward

Maxwell. Will would have cut off his own hands to be free.

He noticed the Tupperware container tucked beneath Maxwell's arm. "You've probably got lots of questions, and there's just so much to tell you," Maxwell said, looking out toward the water. "But not much time."

Will shouted, straining to move the dead weight beneath him. Wisteria vines cut into his wrists. The cords were knotted well. He couldn't budge them. It occurred to him with clarity that he was about to die. His body would soon become garbage on the beach, to be picked slowly apart by marine life.

Maxwell unsnapped the lid of the Tupperware container. "I see you've been digging through Howard Mansell's dossier," he said, removing a photo from the container.

"You killed him. You killed that boy's father," Will said, pulling upward as the waters rushed past him, sandblasting his face. Salt water invaded his mouth and nostrils, gagging him.

Maxwell turned over the Tupperware container, spilling its contents into the ocean. "Do you know about this place? In all your snooping, did you learn anything about the Crescent? It's been here a long time, Will. And the funny thing is, nobody can figure out how these big rocks even got here. They're not from native geologic materials, you understand. It's like they just sort of fell from outer space."

"What about Argus?" Will said. "Why did you kill him? He didn't do anything to you."

"Esther wouldn't go for the whole marriage idea if the officiating pastor were a stark raving lunatic. Didn't sit right with her. But you... oh, she was very happy to see you. Just as I predicted, you were the perfect fit. When West told me about you, I knew it was meant to be."

As Will stared up at Maxwell, these revelations unfolding, it all became very clear. The answer had been there all along. "You're selling Muskogee to Arch Holdings. You did all this for money."

Maxwell leaned down. "A whole shitload of money. About ten million dollars, after I compensate Frederick and Sally for their services. After all, they've earned it."

Will spat in his face. Maxwell wiped it away.

"Everybody has to find their talents," said Maxwell. "They have to use those talents to make their way in life. You've got your . . . expertise. I've got mine. I've always been able to spot the inevitable in every situation."

"But you didn't have to kill people. They were innocent."

"Yes, and that was all very unfortunate," Maxwell sighed. "It couldn't have been avoided, though. The inevitable, Will. You look for it in every situation. The imaginative nature of capitalism would have found a way to take this island off the hands of the late Esther Campbell, with or without my help. This way she gets what she would have wanted."

"What she would have wanted?" Will spat.

"For her beloved to inherit this beautiful island, to do with as I saw fit. And now that it's official, I'll be taking the new will and marriage license to the Chatham County Probate Court. Your signature made it official. We'll let some time pass before notifying the Coast Guard to search for her body. I believe they'll determine it's a lost cause. She never should have gone for that early morning swim."

Will yanked at the vines, kicking at Maxwell.

"Can't you see your situation, Will?" said Maxwell. "Let me make it easier for you. What is inevitable here? Think about it, then embrace it, no matter how ugly it might seem. Because that's the only truth in this sick world."

Will shook his head. "But the journal. The notepad in your bedroom."

"Yes. I thought you might have found that. It never hurts to document what happened, even if it didn't actually happen. You never make a paper trail unless you want to lead someone down the wrong path. Then it becomes quite useful. It's insurance. Frederick had been watching you and John snooping around. Did you really expect to find something? Do you think I'm going to conveniently go and write down my plans to marry a rich heiress, get rid of her, take her land and sell it?"

Will screamed, gritting his teeth. Blood seeped from his wrists as he tore at the vines. "Why me?"

"West gave me your whole story. You're perfect. We had planned on letting you live, but just in case you stepped out of line, we knew we could make you disappear. Who would miss you? And since you happened to see the body of my beloved, you left us no choice." He glanced down at his watch. "It's almost high tide. You've been useful, Will Fordham. I am truly sorry it had to come to this, but you brought it on yourself."

⌒

The minutes passed slowly. Each wave splashed higher than the last as they lapped at his neck. He rose up, pulling Esther with him. He could hear ghost crabs moving inside her skull. He felt them skittering beneath rock-hard dead flesh. Sickening sounds came from her throat. Her lips touched the edge of his earlobe. It was like some gurgling whisper as a crab climbed out of her mouth and scuttled its way up Will's hair. Its distended, black insect eyes examined Will. It looked like a monster this close up. Its alien mouth opened sideways, tiny hairs bristling with motion. Will shook off the crustacean. It landed with a tiny splash in the tide pool.

The waters rose higher and higher. One wave overtook his whole body and left him beneath the surface, sucking in salt water. He gasped, rising up, coughing violently. Polaroids of Howard Mansell floated past him like tiny boats spinning in the surf. The pictures disappeared under the next wave, which was much larger than the others. Will was ready for it this time. He held his breath, blowing out through his nostrils as the water crashed against him, sand peppering the skin of his face.

What was worse, he wondered: the idea that there was no God, or the notion that God did exist and he was a deity of gore? A great, impersonal "it" in the sky dispensing catastrophe on a helpless world trying to make sense of it all. People always said things like "God has a plan" or "He works in mysterious ways."

Oh yes, he has a plan, Will thought as he stared up at the sky. But there's no mystery about it. God's plan is terrifying. No one is exempt from the pain, the carnage of this life, this series of moments that stretch out as if they'll never end until they finally do. So eternal, and so abrupt.

He twisted his fingers, trying to find the knot beneath Esther's wrists. He nearly broke his right hand contorting his own wrist. Beneath her cold, hard hands he felt the rough surface of one of the large rocks. Using all his strength, he pulled upward on the stone, trying to budge it.

He was running out of time. Exhausted and broken, he tried to take comfort in the fact that it would soon be over. Death would be painful but quick enough. In desperation, he prayed. He asked for God or whoever was listening to take him to heaven if such a place did exist. As the final moments of consciousness faded away, he longed for nothing more than to see Aaron again.

Another photo floated past: a picture of Howard Mansell and his infant son, John. The photo spun in the surf before currents pulled it back into the ocean. Will prayed again, this time that God would perform some miracle and he could rescue John. He had to tell him what he'd seen. He had to tell John that he believed him, and he was sorry for ever doubting.

The next wave nearly killed him. He was underwater for what felt like hours. He coughed, shaking. He was nearly blinded by the sand that blasted his eyes. The pain was awful.

A lone voice sounded out over the crashing waves. It was the voice of a young boy calling out to him. Had God granted one of his prayers?

<hr>

John arrived at Will's side, wading through knee-deep water. "You've got to get out of here," Will shouted, rising up. "They're going to see you."

John knelt in the crashing surf. Plunging an arm into the water, he grabbed Will's wrist. There was a sudden stabbing pain in Will's hand, and he shouted.

"Sorry," John said, trying to keep still as the waves crashed over him. A very large wave sent him sprawling past Will, the boy's head disappearing beneath the water. Will shouted John's name, craning his neck to see if the boy was okay. Why had John come out here? Maxwell or Frederick would surely see him, and then both of them would end up dead. He scanned the waters, looking for him. It felt all too much like déjà vu. How many children did he have to see drowned in this life? How many people who depended on him would he have to fail before it all came to an end? Even as his own life seemed to be coming to an end, the misery persisted.

John emerged suddenly from the waters, coughing. He waded back toward Will, reaching again for his wrist. Several moments later, Will's left hand was free. John had cut the vine—and Will—with his father's lock blade. Will took the knife from John and cut the binds from his other hand, and then he cut the vines from around his ankles. Will briefly examined his hand where John had accidentally cut him. Blood oozed from the puncture wound. It looked bad.

"Mrs. Esther," John gasped, pointing. The dead woman bobbed beside them. When cutting the vines, he'd also freed her from the rocks. Her body tumbled in the rushing waters, tossed by the waves.

"We've got to get to the pier," Will said. "The boat might still be there."

Pocketing the knife, he grabbed John's hand. John turned his frightened eyes toward Will. "It's okay," Will said. They sprinted together up the beach as storm clouds pelted them with rain. Thunder cracked in a deafening explosion. Jagged fingers of lightning flashed beyond the trees ahead.

When they reached the sand dunes, Frederick was there waiting for them. The pit bull paced circles in the sand behind Frederick, ears flattened, whining. The animal was terrified. Stark shivered, cowering as thunder clapped.

Will whispered to John, "I'll meet you there."

"I won't leave you," John said.

"Go!" Will shouted. "Now!"

Frederick strode toward them. Will lunged first, tackling Frederick. The two men hit the sand, each landing a flurry of punches. Swinging an elbow into Frederick's face, Will heard a loud crunch.

Frederick's nose exploded with blood. Will struck again. The right hook rattled Frederick. Will's knuckles stung from the blow.

He hadn't been in a fight since high school, when he'd been forced to defend himself against someone picking on him between classes. He'd felt the rage rising, clouding all his thoughts as he became something like an animal. A large crowd had gathered in the hallway, watching the metamorphosis of this quiet boy who suddenly seemed bent on killing.

He felt that way now as Frederick crawled back to his feet. He spit blood in the sand. With a running start, he charged. Will dodged him, and then hit Frederick in the ribs. The blow halted Frederick. Will swung again, imagining the punch going straight through the back of the man's skull. John was still there, watching them, waiting for the right moment.

Frederick staggered backward. He laughed, wincing. "You've got some fight in you."

They clashed again, and John made a run for it.

"Hey!" Frederick called out, seeing John cut past them. Will grabbed Frederick around the neck and locked his arms together, squeezing off the air supply. Leaning back, he tightened his bicep around Frederick's throat, but the huge man lifted Will off the ground, tossing him into the sand. Will got up fast, feeling the adrenaline coursing. Feeling no pain, only hatred. He attacked Frederick again, landing another round of blows. He felt possessed by a powerful contempt that seemed to guide his hands, giving strength to each fist as he crushed Frederick's face.

All at once, Frederick's knees buckled, and he fell. He looked up at Will, the flesh of his mouth splayed and bloody. "Goddamn," he muttered, unsheathing a large hunting knife. He stood, making a weak run at Will.

Will flipped John's lock blade out of his pocket and made fast slashes, producing a swift, sickening sound against Frederick's midsection. His eyes registered shock as he looked down at his torso. Frederick clutched at his stomach. The wound was terrible. Frederick backed away, shaking his head. He tried to cover the wound but blood pulsed out between his fingers. It soaked through his shirt, dripping. It darkened the sand beneath him.

Will didn't wait around to see what happened. He made a run up the sand dunes. He sprinted with what little energy he had left. After several minutes, he spotted the trail that led to the pier. With a little luck, John would be there waiting with Amos, the boat captain.

Tree branches swayed in the wind. The storm was reaching new levels of intensity. He entered the forest path, sneakers pounding the dirt. Lightning popped. Thunder rumbled low in the distance.

"You killed him," a voice shouted.

Will stopped. He pulled out the knife, flicking it open. Was he hallucinating again? He turned left and right, peering into the forest. He didn't have time for this now. He had to get to John before it was too late. He had to get to the boat. There was no escape otherwise. It was no time for his mind to play tricks. The knife wound on his palm screamed in pain. His whole hand was slippery with blood. He couldn't tell whether it was Frederick's or his own.

Maxwell stepped out from behind a tree. "You know, I didn't want to have to kill you myself. I'm not a murderer. I preferred a simpler way of making you disappear." He frowned disapprovingly. "I guess the storms will carry your body so far it won't matter."

Will dashed toward him, raising the knife. He would kill this man.

He would rid the world of an evil so black nobody could fathom it.

Maxwell leveled a pistol at Will's head, the big Smith & Wesson that Frederick had used to kill the hog.

All at once, strange sounds filled the air. The squawking of birds, the rustling of bushes, wild animals calling out with hellish noises from all around. Will felt a release of pressure in the air, but also inside of himself. He shook with an unexplainable sensation, as if one hundred pounds of rusty chains had suddenly dropped from his arms and legs. Trembling, he gazed toward the sky. A swirling wisp of white cloud unfurled above. Behind it, a dark procession of clouds a mile wide. A flock of large fowl exploded from the underbrush, filling the tree branches. A bobcat screamed. A herd of hogs bolted through the woods.

Maxwell turned for a split second, startled. Will didn't hesitate. He grabbed the muzzle of Maxwell's pistol with one hand. With the other hand, he sank the lock blade into Maxwell's shoulder. Maxwell cried out, clawing at the knife.

A gunshot rang out. A sensation like fire ran up the length of Will's arm. Will looked down to see that the pistol had blown a hole through his palm. His pinky finger dangled sickeningly by a thread of flesh. Pieces of bone were visible. Blood streamed from the gaping wound. With his other hand, Will seized the pistol from Maxwell and aimed it at the old man's face.

A low rumbling flooded his skull with a horrifying noise. A numbing cocktail of adrenaline pulsed through his body. Maxwell looked over Will's shoulder, mouth agape. The old man stumbled backward, eyes filling with horror.

Will dropped the gun and ran. He knew what was coming. He'd known it since the beginning. Here it was.

CHAPTER FOURTEEN

He hurdled past Maxwell, whose eyes bulged as he clutched at the knife buried in his shoulder. Will ran hard, his whole body pumping as he scanned the landscape for something to brace against. He darted down the dirt trail, wet sneakers slapping the ground. As Will moved, he became aware of a louder crashing sound in the woods. He saw animals of all kinds, creatures he didn't think inhabited the island: a herd of deer pranced with urgency, two gray foxes dashed, and dozens of rats scurried along the forest floor. Palm fronds rattled with dozens of skittering green lizards.

All the creatures ran inland, seeking shelter from the towering wave which rushed at them like a liquid wall. Will hobbled to a stop. He could hear the water closing in. There was no time. Wrapping his body around the trunk of a live oak, he locked his arms together, bracing for impact.

The sixteen-foot-tall wave hit like an explosion, upending Will's body, twisting his back. Something popped inside him, and he cried out in pain. Despite this, he held on tightly to the tree trunk. He rode out the surging waters. Eyes squinted in agony, he worked his way up the tree. He climbed underwater for what seemed like an eternity.

His head felt like it was going to explode. Consciousness was slipping away. His body seemed to move automatically, continuing to climb. But everything was going black.

He broke the surface, gasping.

Will emerged on a new Muskogee Island, one made of water and treetops. Gripping the oak's gnarled branches, he looked around. A bolt of lightning danced across the horizon. Thunder jarred him. He hugged the tree tightly, but his body was tired, his breaths ragged.

Will didn't even know if John could swim. He hoped the boy had gotten to the pier in time. A sickening fear clutched at his heart as he scanned the surface for anything recognizable. A whole tree tumbled past him end over end, its root system rising from the surface like an aquatic monster.

He spotted the top of a building, which he immediately recognized. It was the chapel. The church bell remained, on a post above the tumultuous waters. He waited, watching for more debris. He needed something big he could float on. Otherwise, he would drown in a matter of seconds. His arms were growing weaker. He couldn't hold on for much longer. His body had been pushed to the limit and beyond. There was also the chance that he was about to bleed to death.

Something large appeared in the distance, pinballing its way through tree branches, hurtling toward him. He climbed higher, watching it approach. Spotting the bright green leaves and the blood-red berries, he realized it was an uprooted yaupon holly bush. Will dropped with a heavy splash, grabbing for the plant.

He rode the prickly holly like an insane watercraft, its base spinning as he tried to stay on top of it. He was approaching the church at a rapid rate. When he was close enough to reach it, he grabbed at a corner of the roof and pulled himself up out of the water. He lay on the red roof like a fish tossed from the stream. He writhed, spitting out water. The bullet wound on his hand flashed with pain, seeping dark blood. He removed his shirt and wrapped it around his mutilated hand, tying a double knot. It would have to do for now. He climbed higher on the steep roof, surveying his surroundings. He knew that the church was the farthest building inland, so he was in the safest place... but the boy.

Will inched his way across the steep rooftop. A fine misting of water coated the metal, making it slick as ice. He slipped once, nearly tumbling, as he made his way toward the church bell, the top of which stuck out of the water by about a foot. To keep from slipping again, he got down on all fours, stretching out toward it. His fingers shook, straining to reach it. Finally, he got ahold of the cord and pulled it. The sound of the bell rang out over the waters. He yanked it again, remembering what Esther had said: You could hear it from anywhere on the island.

The whole church shifted. He heard the sound of wood splintering, of windows cracking. The building was about to come down beneath him. The waves were taking it apart piece by piece. The decrepit old chapel could only take so much.

Will thought he heard something in the distance. Like the rumble of a boat's motor, he hoped. He scanned the horizon, looking through the tangle of tree branches, but saw nothing on the open waters, which continued to rise. Water lapped at the sanctuary's roof, each wave inching closer to Will.

The tin roof boomed suddenly behind Will, startling him. He heard wet gurgling sounds. He turned and saw Maxwell. The old man's mouth gaped open, sucking desperately for air. Waters rushed around the two men as they faced each other. The current was still violently strong. The roof would soon be underwater. "You...you've brought this," Maxwell gasped, clutching his shoulder. Fresh blood streamed between his fingers.

Maxwell lunged at him, snarling. Will grabbed him by the throat, slamming him against the steep tin roof. His eyes bulged, mouth working open and shut like a gasping fish. Between his hands, Will pinched the man's skinny neck even tighter.

Will felt no sympathy, only hatred, as he squeezed. He wanted murder.

Maxwell kicked free. With his fingernails, Maxwell clawed at the hole in Will's hand. He spit blood in Will's face, sliding from his grasp. The sound of rushing waters intensified, and both men turned. A large wave suddenly crashed against them. Both lost their balance. Maxwell went down hard, grabbing Will's leg as he hit the slick surface. The building buckled, sinking into the ocean.

They tumbled together into the rushing waters.

Upon hitting the surface, Maxwell lost his hold on Will and vanished beneath the swift current. Will grabbed at the church bell post. He reached out, ringing it once, then twice, before the rope slipped out of his hand. He swam hard, arms and legs pumping. His body was spent. He couldn't stay above the surface. In a panicked moment, he sucked in a mouthful of ocean water. Pain spread in his skull as the salt water invaded his lungs. His sight grew dim. Lightning popped. Thunder rumbled. The world went black and white. Someone screamed his name. The woeful shouts sounded like delirious laughter.

And then, light. A hand cut the surface above, plunging toward him. Fingers outstretched, beckoning. The hand of a child.

EPILOGUE

From the Savannah Daily Post
August 28, 2015

FOURTEEN MISSING, FEARED DEAD, ON MUSKOGEE ISLAND
Heiress Among Deceased in Storm

Storms that ripped through the coast as a result of Tropical Storm Anna may have taken the lives of more than a dozen Muskogee Island inhabitants. Surging waters covered the island yesterday afternoon, rising more than 20 feet.

Despite the perilous conditions, two people were miraculously saved by a courier-boat captain combing the waters. Local Coast Guard officials said the rescuer, Amos McGuire, 36, of Savannah, was arriving to pick up materials from the island's artist colony, when he saw a boy on the pier.

"Mr. McGuire indicated that the boy was trying to get his attention," said Coast Guard spokesman Butch Kimball. "When the boy stepped onto the vessel, the storm made its full impact."

Kimball said McGuire and the child, whose name has not been released, began to hear a bell ringing. "There's a church toward the middle of the island," he said. "The flooding at this point was such that they were able to navigate their way to the source of the sound, where they located the second survivor."

William Fordham, 30, of Savannah had climbed to the top of the small chapel. He suffered critical injuries during the storm surge. Kimball said Fordham is currently in stable condition at an area hospital, where he is expected to survive.

While Tropical Storm Anna did not make landfall on Savannah, its effects were felt in the way of heavy rains. "It's not uncommon for a storm surge to occur," said local meteorologist Bill Richard. "But it is unusual for one of these to flood an entire island. My thoughts and prayers go out to the family members of those lost."

Few were recovered during the Coast Guard's search. Of the estimated 14 people who were still missing, only two bodies were identified: Esther Campbell, 68, and Maxwell Summerour, 64.

Known publicly for her philanthropic spirit, Campbell was recently the subject of media attention due to her plans to donate Muskogee Island to the Georgia

Department of Natural Resources for green space. It was reported in past editions of the Daily Post that developers from several companies had approached her over the years, also offering to purchase the land. Department of Natural Resources Commissioner Lex Bodan confirmed that the island would likely become DNR property. Campbell had no surviving relatives, but she had made arrangements for the island's ownership to pass to the state agency in the event of her death.

Those who lived on Muskogee Island were members of an artist colony, established by Campbell several years ago following the death of her husband. She invited artists to stay on the island as a "service to the community."

"That's just who she was," Bodan said. "She was a kind woman with a big heart. Her philanthropy knew no limits. We are deeply saddened by this troubling news, but we hope to help fulfill what she made clear was her wish, that Muskogee Island remain pristine."

ACKNOWLEDGMENTS

For Joy, Stella, Mom, Dad, Wayne, Linda, Matt, Shawn, Chris, Duncan, Neil, Chris Martin, Tyler, Stephen, and the Gill Clan.

Special thanks to Charles Duncan, Tom Sauret, Jim Chapman, Dan Cabaniss, Jason Mosser, Kevin Atwill, Keith Albertson, Todd Cline, and Kristen Iskandrian for having taken the time to teach.